WILLMS ROAD
COLLECTED SHORT STORIES

Michael R. Häack

authorHOUSE®

AuthorHouse™
1663 Liberty Drive
Bloomington, IN 47403
www.authorhouse.com
Phone: 833-262-8899

Published by AuthorHouse 10/21/2022

ISBN: 978-1-6655-7160-9 (sc)
ISBN: 978-1-6655-7159-3 (e)

Library of Congress Control Number: 2022917853

CONTENTS

ACKNOWLEDGEMENTS

Dawn Gardner: Content editor
Josh Nagtalon: Book cover photographer
Warren Haack: Book cover graphic designs
Kregg Miller: Business management
Christy Mantz: My daughter who encourages me to write

WILLMS ROAD

Willms Road; a piece of black scratched onto the landscape, stretches south and east from Knights Ferry, California toward Turlock Reservoir. To her glory one could say of Willms that she is mostly straight. You can go to sleep riding down Willms and for certain arrive at the end…but safely? Well, perhaps not. The lay of the land is horst and graben. The narrow county maintained road has a finish akin to the back of a Wild Boar: tough, rough and unpredictable. There is nothing to see along the way that will interrupt your thinking. You can think safely but stay alert; it's primitive!

On a good summer day, with the temperature about 120F on the asphalt road surface and the air dead calm, it's a harsh place to drag yourself and your bike; a place to pant and gasp. I do it if only to avoid the awful realization that otherwise I might never suffer in such a way in this lifetime. On a good day, in the thick of summer, I have taken my bike along Willms and met no one. I will not say I met nothing. That would be a small lie.

Things exist along Willms, things I suspect that God could not fit into other applications on the earth; therefore He parked them along Willms and happily forgot them. Small things abound: tarantulas, coral snakes, turkey buzzards, scorpions and the bleached bones of…other things. There are no fences on Willms. Why bother? Any ill-fated livestock had met a sudden last round-up at a dried-up watering hole. On a scorching day I have spotted, on distant dried stubble hillsides fuzzy-brown hides, fly blown and stretched over brittle bones. Under nicer circumstances they might have passed for cattle. Facing the east as I passed, they left no droppings, passed no water and ate nothing. Nothing exists to eat anyway. The ground, hard as obsidian, has never grown a stick, a twig, or a leaf.

I digress.

On a midnight past, in a fit of traveling fever, I was moved to gain the higher ground. Bent on a bike ride into the bush, I happened upon Willms. No friend about for company, I set off alone. I ventured into moonless black to match the inside of any cow around. There were none. The night lent a new meaning to onerous. I placed the black of tire rubber against the black of asphalt and pressed against the black of night and the onset of time. Ahead, far ahead, rested the other end. Between us, time, tension, and unknown darkness.

Daytime on a bike is for the light of heart and the free of spirit. Nighttime, on the other hand, is a crazy way to wreck the cycle, maim the body and scare life away. I was well experienced with all three. In blackness past I cycled over Monitor Pass, Luther Pass, Kit Carson Pass, not to mention Sonora Pass and Tioga Pass, many times each. Mines Canyon twice survived my tires in dark of night, also Devils Gate, Walker Creek Canyon, Coulterville to Smith Station, and Annie Green Springs to Yosemite.

In the blackest of nights on a west-side descent of Monitor Pass a group of us on bikes hit a porcupine. The bikes survived; the tires and the porcupine, not so well.

I have cycled in a blinding late afternoon downpour from Zermatt, Switzerland to Saint Gilogolph, France. Several times I have climbed and descended Old Priest Grade in full darkness. Willms, however, would teach me a new blackness.

A song is good for a start. With the passing of the first miles and the air white-hot even in the black, I became inspired and broke into hymns. Ironically, the best I could do was *Nearer My God to Thee*. Perhaps not the bravest choice. Later I digressed to, *Up From the Grave He Arose*. My final selection, just prior to hitting the first dead animal was, *We Shall All Be Together By and By*.

Thump! And then *Crash!*

Well, it hurt and for sure scared me. But more than that, there was something scurrying about underfoot! If it bites, I'm dead, if it spits poison pus or emits a killer stench, then ditto. Calm did not exist. I made a muck-up of locating my bike and ran with it in my arms down the road for about 100 yards.

Now understand, in daylight I don't typically break into terror and thrash about on a public road; act a bit odd, well yes, but this was out and out blubbering. I was petrified. I might never know what I hit that night. However, the matter that clung tenaciously to my tires was neither plant nor animal. In the interest of getting ahead of what it was, I continued, but slower now. Small hills appeared like ghostly ramparts and blocked my view of the black road ahead. I would drop off the bike, lean it against my leg and stare hard into…the coal pit before me.

Above, all was well with the heavens. Each star was in place, the black background went well with the earth below and the moon…oh no, I had picked the final waxing of the moon. No warm lunar glow would strike a path for my each step tonight. I was to wander, lost, a mortal awash in his sins, his fanatics, his self- made plight. The festering black encroached on my spaces. I moved on, but slowly, more slowly.

There, now, do you see it? I say, Do – You – See – It?

A movement in the black, like the curtain of coal has shifted ever so slightly and in its place has left a blackness even denser than before. My eyes ached with straining to see…what? I had seen something ahead, out there.

Perhaps the depths of my spirit had at last grown tired of being brave and had given up the struggle. Perhaps this is how it ends: *Brave men the last wave by, they did not go gentle into that good night.* (Thank you, Dylan Thomas) I had lost any "brave" I might have ever possessed. I had joined Shakespeare's "St. Crispin's Day" brigade and was one of his …*sorry gentlemen yet abed in England might think themselves accursed that they were not here, and hold their manhood cheap…* Yep, that's me, cheap manhood, and oh I wished I were abed in England, or Bangladesh, or even Delhi. There, again, now I know for sure…something huge is out there, and it's moving this way, slowly!

I do not have much hair on my body, just enough to pick up a breeze, clutch some sweat or under circumstances such as these, to stand straight up and tremble. Perhaps the hair shook; perhaps the body shook the hair.

None the less, I had to hold tight to the bike for fear of setting off the big *8.1* we in California all await in dread.

Now I gave up on the image of a real man and just plain burst into tears of fear. At first they simply joined my facial contortions of aghast driven by gravity to earth below. But in the later stages I had a much hardened stare of horror on the facial portion.

Shelly stated in <u>Ozymandias</u>, ...*yet remained these characteristics chiseled on his visage, the hand that mocked them and the heart that fed...*

I suspect the horrorstruck look was chiseled into the mud God lent to my mug at creation, and the tears of fear had washed away any likeness of the human *visage* that had once been. The remains weathered now into a piece of naked, bleached driftwood; adrift indeed, in the seas of time, space and emotions.

After a few years on a bike, (I had been on bikes doing extended rides since 1959), a person becomes rather used to what happens on any road at any given time. As you go along, hit bumps, cushion for them, shift gears for hills and leaps, change seat positions and handlebar positions for climbs and descents, one tends to make such changes which allow one to suffer less as time goes on.

In the first hour on a bike it's usually bliss and laughter. Later on it's work and tedium. Further along the day is stressful and one approaches anger at each bump and climb. Then will come that famous *leap* when you descend and get a wind-assisted rush downhill. At last there is a dreaded *drip-stage* when all energy is gone, the legs become vacuums, the mind weeps for comfort and parts of the body drop off and are instantly captured in the rear wheel and are driven to ground. These are the strange smudge marks you see on the pavement each day when zipping past in an auto at fifty-five mph.

Once in a descent from Yosemite National Park through Merced River Canyon, I fell asleep past tiny Briceberg in the 14th handlebar position, leaning on forearms and dangling hands down dangerously toward the front spokes. As I went to sleep my left hand slid down into the front wheel and broke a finger in the spinning spokes.

Later, on that same cold winter's ride, a stretch cord on my rear rack broke and off flew a loaf of bread and a small bottle of wine. Quite possibly they attended to the needs of some riders who passed later on, and enjoyed the first ever Eucharist on the highway.

Willms Road has a way with the rider. You can ride that seventeen miles and never have a real experience. You can also get over with all the experiences of a lifetime in just a fast first mile or two. Tonight was to surpass all previous records.

One wants for a few comforts in life: on a cold winters eve it's a fireside and a warm cuppa. Perhaps on a cool afternoon a sunny window seat and a spot of the grape will do. On a bike out in the bush it's always nice to have the weather fine and a hot sun on the back. Meanwhile, on a cool evening, one cranks harder and looks for a mild gradient to generate warmth.

This night was an exception. It was hot, dark and worrisome too. One wanted a long-sleeved jersey against the darkness, not against the temperature. The body wanted a shield, something to make the aura comfortable. Sun-tanned skin fails me at times like this. The God-given wrapper is too thin, too transparent, and too vulnerable. In times like these I cry out to the heavens for a mantle against my most unknown dreads. In place I receive darkness and goose bumps. So, well I can imagine, how those before me suffered, persevered, perished for that alone which I will search the dark for: a spark of life, a ray of warmth, a hand that holds, and in my searching will I realize my own flesh is weak and thin against life's *slings and arrows of outrageous fortune*. (Thank you Mr. Shakespeare.)

I move ahead. I could turn back about, return to a known path, a lighter place, the warmth of known civilization. That would never do. To give up is a message to life to turn about and give less in each day's serving: less light, less dark, less pain, less accomplishment, less tedium and less astonishment. To gain less in any area of the battle is to forfeit the gain in all areas; as in Ecclesiastes, *There is nothing new under the sun*.

We will visit the last flashing sky, see stones fall all day, feel the bite of cold seas arrival, and glimpse open pits of earth's inner furnace-forced breath. And yet, we will have seen nothing that has not been seen by others before. What we must realize for each man's being, what we aspire to, new or forever repeated, is in how we attack and accomplish our challenges. Therefore, onward I will advance against that blackness which has been new to me, but may glove the pent-up burdens of a million past glances, painful or in joy divine.

I pressed against the wall of black and the night of gloom. Now the curtain was down against the tarmac. There was not a spark of light from stars above, and no gleam of night-time animal eyes to foretell of watchers in the dark. Making a lone path into night's maw was what my future held.

Ahead, in a gasp of realization, I beheld the maddened road become *elevator patches* of asphalt. Played upon a keyboard, this rise and fall would pluck out a version of some unnamed composer's *Song of Night's Death*.

I wanted no part of this, and yet I was the invited guest of honor. For me, the road was alive with jumping globs of the blackness. For my own entertainment did the plates of earth rise and fall, shift and dive. For my eyes alone did space and time seem to mix into a seemingly endless turmoil of hiccupping hilltops.

I rode on.

The bike seemed to become a part of the muck underfoot. The tires, once round and firm with pounds per square inch of air, were now just a black extension of the endless *conveyor belt* of roadway. I was the object to be manipulated.

Time stood alone. Everything about it moved in a madness of thrusting and withdrawing. I was a rat in a maze, a yoyo on a string, an insect on a web, a blubbering gimbal entwined with bent metal.

The pace increased. My experiences on a bike tell me I am headed with all dispatch downhill. This is not a lovely curve downward to a calm, gardened edge. No, I'm on that blinding rush aliken to down *Old Priest Grade*, out of any controls applied to logic and safety.

The pavement has attacked bike and rider again. Now we face blackened deleterious hillocks of mud and grime. The road becomes a millrace of quickened nerve endings and blanched emotions. To bike downhill is still an event to behold. The same thing, out of control, is a horrid nightmare. When the rubber is melted into a mush of black and the frame slides into supine posture, only then will the rider be the last one to have any say in the ride's end. It has taken a turn into a sunset of the blackened underside of a mud wall.

Above, all is dark. No hope there. Below, well into the earth, resides a fiend of horrors who lifts the pavement at random and I play hopscotch with enraged asphalt. Now the patch of black shifts left and right. There, ahead, the curtain lifts again. The exposed remains of eve's sky is tossed against that black gasp of midnight's touch.

I must awaken. Too long out of touch is a sure path to infinite madness. In a dream, Feodor Dostoyevsky placed his *Ridiculous Man* to face his own nightmares, his own haunts and fears. Well into my ages and perhaps my cups now, I too must face those endless night's dreams. Pallor of face but indeed a readiness of spirit. I lapse nightly into an infirmity of senselessness

Now barnyards of ramparts and dead cattle, then it's fields of runaway freight wagons filled with water. One night I fancy myself floating face up in water, a dead fish, the next night, adrift on escalator shafts of freezing airs and I become the hunted bird-on-the-wing with blazing shells erupting from each tree and bush. But this, what dream do I depict now? Must I face this banishment to madness nightly for eternity?

I glance at my watch. Perhaps the night is well gone and dawn's warming love is nigh and will soon embrace me. I am aghast; more horror to endure as the watch indicates 12:17, exactly the time I mounted my bike to begin this plague! Time was standing still. In my anxiety I have received a most dreaded and endless course of terror garbed in more revolting revulsion.

Against the night I rest my labored body and fair steed. Against the darkness I pause and press far into years to come. I look for myself at peace, perhaps in green fields by a brook. I fancy a laughing lady, and well overhead, birds at song caroling me to eves-rush home. I am happy in this vision; it fits my needs.

It shall not fit this gown I stand draped in now, this mantle of gloom resting like lead on my spent frame. Dickens voices his horror through

Jacob Marley, *I wear the chain I forged in life, of my own free will I wear it. I made it, link by link and yard by yard.* He was sent, a messenger of the mistaken trust in all whom he represented in life. His messages to the world represent what you believe in. Only, put your beliefs in a value far greater than money and wealth of the flesh. Where will my stone lie? And upon it, cast in what brief glimpse of my life, will words attest? *"He rode his bike and went nuts!"*

Is my end so pointless? Do I beckon no more to the good done by self as to be a knot of mud, a stand of dead cattails, or perhaps a spent wick end, in the half-flashed drippings dish?

No, now I say damnation no! I will be more, I shall do more, and I have pushed into a deeper layer: a handsome spot among dwellers on earth reserved for ones who keep the watch. I shall not take lightly the touch of so bleak a countenance on my stone. I will not *go gentle into that good night*, or into any night, good or preposterously distressing!

Speed is always relative to some fixed object. I glance about for that which would let me know that I was either at rest or in flight. My mind sped forth into what was ahead. I demanded the body to be finished, to be at the end, to be resting safely. The bicycle could attend or not; but I was in want of a safe-house, in a blackness of night so deep nothing wills to be "first up." History tells the reason for so tardy a respite. "The last man out burns the forest," and "The devil takes the hindmost," or "The tag end of nighttime harbors the worst of black and cold." Well said, and neither for weaker flesh nor humble limbs. I long for the road to drop me toward the river, toward a familiar bridge, toward the end of trial. Turned to tumult, turned to terror.

More to the bad, no relief in sight; for, in fact, there is no sight. The senses have given up all but the feel of wind on flesh. Onward to no known victory, races the bike, and clinging like cobwebs in a tsunami is flailing flesh gone cold. The event will win and the modus will survive…but no rider will bear witness. He is struck dumb:

> Wheels singing hard times come
> 'gainst roadbed seen better grace.
> Clothing now past rumpled ruin,
> with rents and open space.

Face all cracked and gone away,
with forlorn bracken ditches.
Hair more white than nuptial snows,
gauntly robbed of life's last riches.

Now taken as a picture whole,
if needs must in fact be taken,
hopes for self from such grim space
wouldst this sad dreamer waken.

Taken as a whole this was not such a sorry event in my life. I have been away from it now for almost six years and, when not in the isolation chamber, can actually address it. Coerced by friends here at the home I have been able to write it all down. I am allowed to visit my family weekly now and at times the matron will go off with me to see my bicycle; although by heavens graces not yet certified stable enough to touch or ride it.

Such events take a spirit from each of us. We are wealthier as a result, albeit less physically and mentally attuned. Why only recently, accompanied of course, I was allowed to visit the place where they discovered my babbling and grossly distorted body; that horrible night now long past.

It is a celebration of sorts and I mindfully take along a lantern against the sudden onslaught of darkness or pestilence. It is a sobering event for a fact. We take the turn off from the 120 Highway onto Willms Road. We travel less than three miles on the road to a bend where a cliff hides all trace of land and distance. It is at this spot they found me deep into that night. I was on the ground with the bike atop my body. They tell me that I was babbling and foaming at the mouth a good deal. I wore no clothes except for my watch and cycling helmet. My watch was still running and it indicated 12:17. It always says 12:17. It is stuck in the warp which released me to a finer fate. I wait for that day in earnest terror, that day when I demand of myself to go out, in daylight of course, and ride that bike again. Just not at night and never on Willms Road.

Note from the author:

> Willms Road does actually exist in the bleakness of the East Stanislaus Plain. It exists and is very much the way I have described it, surviving in much the way I have ridden it, quite often for at least 55 years. I have ridden it only once at night. Sadly I might never ride Willms Road or any other road again, unless they release me from the home.

THANKSGIVING IN THE DEEP

"**N**ow hear this! Now hear this…"
The message came over the squawk box in our barracks, U.S. Naval receiving station, San Diego at about 0900 hours. Within 30 minutes we were on a military bus enroute to the naval submarine births at Coronado, California.

Nervous minutes later we were ensconced inside our multimillion-dollar steel tube, and, following the usual getting underway routine, we dropped below, began to add pressure and take on water ballast while heading north and west toward Channel Islands; then deeper into the broad blue Pacific. We maintained a slow dive until midday, then leveled off at our designated cruise depth at about 1300 hours. (1 pm, for all you land lubbers.)

My grandparents stood beside their dark green Lincoln Continental and stared at the empty berthing slot located in the deep-water channel, which runs between San Diego and Coronado. They looked at the spot, where only hours earlier, was berthed my submarine, now just deep, dark water. They were confused, slightly worried and just a little bit angry too.

I had taken them to see the site the day before and reminded them that they were to be my guests the next day at 1300 hours for Thanksgiving dinner; an honor not often bestowed on civilians. However, owing to how few crew remained onboard on that holiday, it was the exception which led me to invite them. And now…the boat was gone. I was gone, without a single word of explanation (a fact of life when serving with the Naval Security Group.)

My grandfather, San Diego city engineer, dropped one of his usual witty comments, "Perhaps they all went fishing," which did little to assuage my grandmother's Irish ire.

Onboard a submarine it doesn't do much good to worry about how far down you are, I mean, in six feet, six meters, or sixty fathoms, water takes its toll just the same. I tried to never consider exactly how much of the dark, wet stuff was overhead, and in this case, while the exact figure was unpublished, there was well over 1000 feet of the non-breathable substance above us.

Our captain had an odd sense of humor in his choice of the music he often piped over the address system; which, in this case, was *The Thunderer* by John Philip Sousa; not a bad choice considering once while deep diving he played *Nearer My God to Thee*! A good skipper, but perhaps just slightly warped. *In the Sweet By and By* was another favorite of his. Considering most often there was only the soft hum of electronics, the background roar of air pressure pumps keeping things dry inside, and way far off the throb of General Electric Boats finest (we were on a diesel electric not a nuclear submarine), propelling us along at a gentle so many knots per hour, I guess the choice of music might have been a good deterrent from the ambient sounds of our steal cylinder; a product of submarine builders superlative welders.

We, in the Naval Security Group, were a small contingent of men; four non-coms and two officers, housed in a tiny compartment with its double-locking hatch, and its own hum of electronic gear. There was the slight smell of ozone, and a soothing background buzz of Morse code flooding the headphones of whoever was standing watch; usually two men but occasionally more jammed inside the tiny space at once.

We copied, day and night, whatever flowed into our carefully tuned earphones and typed it onto multiple layers of paper.

On that day, as we departed the calm of a safe harbor, and all forms of ship-to-shore lines, Thanksgiving dinner was to be served onboard the sub at about 1700 hours, late but delicious none-the-less. At most times, submarine food was considered the very best in the entire navy. I can second that, although I was always hungry and there was not too much navy food I disliked, aside from Salisbury steak, liver, and avocados. I always hated avocados, so it shocked my mother, who adored them, when I wrote home to inform her that it was typical in a navy chow line that there were tubs of half avocados being served. She was aghast. As for the other two, I never cared much for meat, but was not yet a vegetarian. However, whatever the two meat items mentioned were made from they smelled like they left the cow without a single cut of the knife, if that garners up the correct image.

That day was the only thanksgiving meal I ate onboard a naval vessel and it was fantastic.

Subs were famous at the time, not only for their scrumptious repast, but even better, they had onboard ice cream making equipment! We traded ice cream in port for things we didn't have, such as movies (the kind you play over a projector as nothing else had been invented at that time.) Ice cream was the coin of the realm, the trade commodity of the era. We could have it three meals a day if we chose. I had it for breakfast a few times with waffles! I can still hear my rather strict grandmother's response, "Well, I never." She, who frequently enjoyed brandied fruits with her breakfast!

We stood watch in the usual three-section rotation, day watch from 0800 'till 1700, eve watch from 1700 'till 0000, and the deadly harsh mid watch of 0000 'till 0800. We stood two of each in a row and always the day to mid was tough, as you got off at 1700 and had to be back at 2345 including eating, talking, sleeping etc.

No one was smart enough to sleep much between those two watches, and also sleeping space was at a premium, and not exactly quiet either. We found an electronics compartment; actually a small storage bay, filled with humming electrical equipment which was warm, not too noisy, and dark. Two off duty watch standers could sleep on the deck unless it became necessary for someone to gain access to the space, then all grief broke out and we quickly left.

We had so little to do onboard, that typically, even when off watch, we hung about in the secure radio spaces anyway. We also went to the general service radio space and showed off our code skills to the radiomen there. Remember that there were no DVDs, VCRs, iPods, iPads, computers, etc. We read books, talked, watched the twice-a- day movie, and slept. We were cleared for top secret, yet were not allowed into any of the spaces onboard except where we needed to be. So all the places I dreamed of going; I never got there: the bridge, Combat Information Center, engine room, forward torpedo room, steering aft, etc.

It was during some of this off-duty boredom time that the game of Kratz and Drugle was invented. It's a game that looks like a cross between chess and the Chinese game of Mahjong. We played it for hours, mostly to amuse each other, and also the less-informed members of the crew in the non-secure radio spaces. We never gave away much information about that game, and to this day I have an original version, plus a new duplicate form which I made, so I could teach my students the finer points of security and scrutiny. Wonderful stuff!

That Thanksgiving day we sat down in groups, as the opportunity arose, to a dinner much like would be offered at home, but lacking my stern mother, my perfect-gentleman dad and my three crazy brothers. With heaps more of everything, there was enough to serve the entire crew, and then some.

The galley had done it right which included decorated dishes, decorated tables, wall hangings and even the line servers were dressed up! I asked if this was unusual and they said, if the situation is calm enough then, no. It's what they like to do to show that even food service is important on a ship (boat) of the fleet.

Everything onboard a submarine is smaller and more compact, housed so it can easily be moved aside to make way for loading and unloading, for rapid passage in times of drills, etc.

If you are reading this with images of *Hunt for Red October*, or *Crimson Tide*, then cut all that down by about two thirds, and you might be at about the right scale for the sub I'm referring to.

As we sat for Thanksgiving dinner that day, more than a few who were not used to being away from home for holidays, were slightly emotional, I know I was. I had planned to sit with my grandparents. Meanwhile my parents and three brothers were sitting down to the typical thanksgiving dinner at home, without me. I suspect they coped. We did, with the help of some crew who dabbed in humor, stories of other holidays aboard vessels and even a few jokes. A blessing was offered by a few hands, and while many were not actually believers, there was a very respectful attitude altogether.

We dined on turkey, ham, chicken, three types of potatoes, vegetables, sauces, gravies and numerous beverages. Of course no alcohol is served onboard a U.S. Naval vessel. (Since 1917.) This was followed by pies: apple, peach, lemon and chocolate cream. There was coffee, tea, lemonade, and of course…Ice Cream, in four flavors! If you didn't get enough to eat that day it was your own fault, or the demands of watch standers on duty. We made it a point to relieve the three who were on our department communications watch for as long as they wished, so they could enjoy the feast too.

Eve watch came and went and it was mid watch time. I was on my string off and stood no watches for two days, during which time I spent most of the hours back in the radio spaces or watching whatever movie was being shown, typically for the umpteenth time. We had a small collection of movies to watch and when they had all been viewed we watched them again and again until we reached port or met up with a carrier or supply ship and traded movies for…Ice Cream, what else?

On a typical cruise, subs could meet up with inbound naval craft and offload mail addressed to loved ones at home. It was slow, but did get there. We were submerged for portions of six weeks and there was no communicating topside. Period.

We were also there for Christmas and New Year's Day, and while it was somewhat sobering to be away from any communications home for all three holidays, it was a fact of the job and the service to the military. You could say "I wish" all you might but the odds of Santa Claus dropping down the forward torpedo-loading hatch was not too likely. (Lord help us if he did. That opening was a direct access to all forward compartments and we would flood and sink in seconds.) He did arrive, however dressed to the beard and all, and lugging a giant bag with cool small gifts for all hands. I think the captain was Santa, and the first officer helped, and I also suspect they paid for the gifts, since no one I have ever spoken to experienced such treatment.

We had small Christmas trees throughout the boat, including the official "Christmas Tree," which was a series of red and green lights indicating all compartments secure and ready to dive. There were lights, music was piped throughout, we had, a Christmas Eve service and another dinner of monstrous proportions, but that's for another story.

This one's finished, and you know, given the chance I would do it all over again, so long as I could survive to meet each of you whom I am blessed with as friends or as family.

I returned to my various land station duties eventually, finished off my four year tour of duty and went off to college. Some men I was stationed with also left for college and job, but some remained onboard subs and ships for a life of service to the United States Navy.

Oh yes, when I attempted to explain the early and unexpected departure to my stern grandmother, her response, which to this day still can crack me up, was, "Well, for heaven's sake, they should have let you call us at least. Don't they have phones aboard those modern submarines?"

A few years after I was discharged, the U.S. Navy Nuclear Submarine *Scorpion* was doing somewhat the same duty, in somewhat the same waters, with some of the same crew I had served with, and was lost at sea with all hands. God alone has a way to comfort those families who lost loved ones in that tragedy. He is an amazing God, and in light of His love and watchful care, I am able to relate this story. I'm here today to celebrate yet another Thanksgiving, and to thank Him for His love, comfort, and supplying me with everything in life; most certainly each of you, who are my loved ones and friends.

> Deep water, steep mountains, harsh winters and blazing desert sunsets; all part of His creation; all gifts given out in generous proportion, and all examples of His love for each of us.

> Hold us in your care until that time when we get to enjoy unity with the greatest gift of them all, your son Jesus Christ.

THE GIRL IN THE
DRIVE-THRU WINDOW

I had followed the arrow to, *Kaffee Drive-thru* and arrived to hear the detached voice from inside the drive-thru speaker. "What can I get started for you?" Soft, lovely, an early-morning voice.

Snow had been falling for three days by then, falling steadily, and, with the outside temperature hovering around 28 degrees; there were a couple of things I would like to have suggested she might start for me.

"Ahh, a large coffee and something hot..." By then I had extinguished the engine so I could hear her remotely musical voice in the tin order box.

"We have breakfast buns..."

I bet you do. "Ok, that would be nice. Two of them, please."

"Thank you, and will you have them warmed?"

That was almost too much for my rapidly-vanishing restraint.

You better believe it...er... "Yes please."

"Thank you. That'll be three and six at the window."

I wound up my side window and set about getting the reluctant machine to start again. It was old, cold, bad tempered and should it block the drive-thru window might become a "target" for the Germans in line behind me. They had a passion for their early morning coffee and a Yankee in an English truck might just be the spark necessary to restart WWII. With a roar, a shudder and a grinding of gears I advanced through deepening snow toward the pickup window. The gearbox needed to be seen to in shop very soon.

And the slow wait began.

As I was already shivering from the snow falling and wind's frigid breath, I figured just about anything warm: soft voice, food or machine, would work. However, the ancient English Land Rover I operated had a typically useless British Black Box heater which, following my frustrated comments and expressive jerks on the controls, put out a cough of warmth and some rather nauseating engine oil stink, but very little in comfort. I switched it off and settled into my down parka, fur hat and thoughts of warm beaches in the Caribbean.

I patiently waited.

Via analog hands and an amazingly illuminated face, the clock on the instrument panel boldly informed me it was already past five AM.

I sat waiting in the drive-thru line, with the engine uncertainly chugging away, and me cautiously hiding thoughts of the lovely Swiss-made girl, Hilda, whose warm radiant face would be waiting in the window to collect my handful of Deutschmarks in exchange for a hot beverage and warm buns, well... breakfast buns. Either way, these were items for which my chilled system hungered.

And I patiently waited.

I would have enjoyed some light jazz to keep me company in my morning commute to the coffee shop and back to work. However, at the time of construction, radios were not being installed in the likes of my work-a-day machine. It mattered little as the engine produced enough noise to fend off the best of German oompah bands anyway.

The wipers continued to turn in a fair job against a steady cold-November snowfall.

And I patiently waited.

I was tempted to park the truck, hike inside and enjoy the warm cozy ambience of this very *Bavarian* coffee house. Totally unlike the ghastly faux American coffee shops back in the states, within this hundred year old Gästehaus would be blazing logs in a great stone fireplace, the gentle drone of German music, the comfort of deep, well-worn leather chairs...and the charming Hilda. Should have thought of that sooner; too late now, I was in the line and my order would soon be delivered at the window by Hilda of the blond hair and freckles, Hilda of the low-cut blouse and delightfully-tight Dirndle, Hilda...

Beep, beep!

I awoke from my dream, engaged the gears and advanced all of one Volkswagen length. Volkswagen, ha! I had owned a few of Germany's *Peoplewagons* and if ever there was a machine with a more underpowered heater than my English *Landy,* it was the VW. That car, made in snow and long-winter country, would happily freeze its occupants to death. (Just an extension of the icy deaths suffered by millions in Germany's WWII concentration camps.) The exception was if you froze to death in a VW it was by your own choice, whereas at Auschwitz the decision was made for you.

And I patiently waited.

Ahead, through the clatter of busy wiperblades and drifting snowflakes, I enjoyed a *Christmas Card* scene of narrow, cobbled streets, stone and timber buildings, steeplecrowned churches and alpine trees, charmingly layered in snow; all silently awaiting acknowledgement. I stamped the scene received, stored it for future enjoyment.

I continued to patiently wait.

Again the line advanced and I slowly grew closer to Hilda and my morning cuppa.

Unlike American drive-thru coffee kiosks, *das Tor,* named for its location near a great stone gate, was a very old-world establishment and often staffed by only two people. Today it was Hilda and Erik, a charming lad who brandished an earring, and in bashful confidence had informed Hilda that he was gay. Hilda, in abashed glee, had shared the "secret" with me.

While the inside crowd seldom exceeded eight or ten customers, the drive-thru on that cold snow-falling November morning, easily stretched to twelve patient motor cars, jeeps, trucks and even one sidecar motorcycle; passenger well tucked down inside her heavy parka and fur collar.

Typical of Europeans everywhere, the German people were used to queues and good-naturedly sat with engines chugging and heaters blasting forth soothing waves of warmth; unless of course you operated an early 60's Land Rover and then you simply buried yourself deeper inside your down parka and ...

Patiently waited.

At last I arrived at the window where the lovely Hilda and my hot cuppa appeared.

"Renee, Renee," (yep, that *is* my name. Thank you, mom.) We need help!" This from an aghast and terrified looking Hilda, still lovely, but stammering and shaking. "Renee, are you armed today?"

I was always armed as part of my job as an armed guard at the nearby Fliegerhorst Erding Air Base.

"Park quick, come inside!" Short, chopped-off words, sputtered in a whispered panic. "We have a problem, come…"

Her voice vanished as her profile was yanked from the window by a darkly-hooded person, who fairly tossed her aside, slammed shut the casement and vanished into the dim reaches of the Kaffee shop.

My wait ended brusquely; no hot cuppa for me today.

What the hell? What was going on inside which necessitated calling on an armed civilian? My focus switched to the scene inside of *das Tor;* conditions as volatile as exploded from Hilda's frantic voice? But for the hysterical look on her face, the frenzy in her voice, I would have driven off and contacted local officials. However, I had to determine what it was which demanded *me* inside and was it even prudent to enter?

The drive-thru was empty ahead of me and I swung around the corner, dropped the gearshift and slid to a stop in a parking slot. I took guarded steps along a snow-clogged walkway and warily advanced to the side entrance. Briefly, I paused to slide my Kimber 45 from its holster and checked that it was cocked and locked while realizing that I was strictly an armed civilian, and except in life-threatening situations was hardly expected to intercede. This was an emergency and appeared life-threatening; I continued. The door opened outward at my tug and abruptly I was inside, far too quickly for what I witnessed.

It was a large room of beamed ceilings, wood tables, leather chairs and logs gently burning within their great stone fireplace. Small lanterns flickered on smooth-plank tables; tables occupied by silent morning coffee drinkers with steaming cups in hand and newspapers at the ready. That's where the normal ended and the scene turned swiftly from every day to every nightmare.

As I entered the shadowy space all heads rotated quickly toward me, eyes briefly alight on me as if I had entered totally naked, then rotated back to the serving counter. It was there that the scene of terror was unfolding. Where a large man in black coveralls, black parka with hood up stood, stood holding Hilda with one hand while brandishing a curved-serrated knife in the other. He was not cutting apart buns, at least not the ones one orders for breakfast. Desperately he enveloped Hilda close to his chest while pressing the menacing blade against her throat in a raging manner.

The girl in the drive-thru window had become the girl with the blade to her throat!

To say he had my full and undivided attention would be an understatement. Erik, on the other hand, appeared astonishingly calm as he hovered behind the counter, holding a bar rag to his mouth, almost as if he had something to say, but thankfully had elected to remain mute. It was doubtful that anything Erik might say, at that moment could help defuse the situation.

It is at this point where Hollywood has it all wrong. That blade was not fake, the blood drops welling up around Hilda's lovey neck were real, and no one whipped out a revolver to quickly end the drama. I stood in the shadows and watched and listened, and hoped no one would give me away as an armed ally come to add fuel to the fire.

Action all around the room had stepped up a notch as Hilda's screams bounced off the candle-lit darkness; as people at the tables shuffled restless feet, and Erik appeared to be messing with the expresso machine behind the counter; oblivious to all that was transpiring about him. I was in no mood for his fastidious nature of cleaning all the time and felt a hostility toward him as I realized something unnerving: Erik had set on the serving counter a tall, steaming beverage, and whether for distraction or in fact out of concern, was asking the crazy knife-man, "...would you like something hot to drink? It might help to calm you a bit?" All spoken in an astonishingly calm English embellished with heavy guttural German.

The knife-man's response was an unprintable expletive fired at the crowd in general with further obscenity directed at Erik. However, the assailant reached for the hot beverage and tipped it to his lips while still forcing the blade against Hilda's lovely neck. As he drank, the force of the blade indented the skin on her lovely throat allowing a slow trickle of blood to ease its way down into her blouse. There was further pause as the first warm swallow of coffee slid down his panting throat...and then he screamed!

"Ahh, scheiss! Ahhhhh!" He tossed the cup away, dropped the knife, staggered forward and vomited a marvelous outward projection toward the astonished crowd and all over poor Hilda who, with the grace of a coryphée, slipped away and dived over the serving counter into Erik's astonished arms.

"Oh, Hilda!" He appeared surprised at how much he enjoyed the warm touch of her slightly sweaty body against his quaking chest.

I caught most of this action while shoving the muzzle of my Kimber into the perp's neck, dressing him in handcuffs and marking the event under control.

"...and now if someone would be so kind as to ring up the Sicherheitspolizei..." I suggested to the yet dumbfounded crowd in general. I was almost finished and, realizing how late it was, decided to head off to work as soon as reinforcements arrived.

The crowd had settled down, the police had removed their captive, Erik and Hilda were tucked into a nearby leather chair in locked rapture and I decided to ask the question still puzzling me.

"So Erik." He turned and I continued. "What did you do to that drink to make the nut with the knife lose control and barf?" I was expecting perhaps an extra hot drink, maybe some salt...

"Oh," he seemed bewildered at my question. "I peed in it!"

For weeks after I never felt the same about my coffee, if Erik brewed it.

MIDNIGHT FEAST

Evening

It was well past midnight when I awoke. Awoke to middle-of-the-night conditions; conditions predictably dark and cold, justly expected for deep winter. However, this particular night there existed an appalling difference from what could be considered normal. On this specific night out of all the dark nights of my 47 years I was hurled directly from dead sleep to war zone with no smooth sailing through the luxuriously slow yawning- awakening which one expects, to which one is accustomed.

Hellishly invading my shocked-awake ears was an all-out battle, a viciously anger-growling and teeth-gnashing devastation which raged all around me; a hideous conflagration discharging a chaotic tumult which evoked within me a solitary thought; terror!Terror consumed me, terror even darker than the inky blackened state-of-the-night.

In it's dimly focused and half-asleep state my mind, as well as my body, came under attack.

Meanwhile my nose was assaulted with an appallingly nauseous stench; a hot sticky smell of musty flesh and of... blood!

Any attempt on my part to resist only pulled tighter the terrible tether accosting me in the blinded posture of night's blackened repose. My futile groping about for a light only resulted in a stark reality, a reality too painful to tolerate.

Enclosed within my trapped body my every tormented nerve stabbed to bony marrow with agonizing veracity while the horrible voice of reality screamed at my accosted mind, "Your legs are gone!"

Bedtime

Nights I resembled a fetal wadded-up bundle in a sleeping bag on the floor of the chamber I shared with a college medical student named Ashton. What might appear as an unusual sleeping posture for most was normal for me. Somehow it was just how I chose to sleep, sort of a full time indoor camping trip, albeit in a most incongruent atmosphere.

The room we occupied was rented from an octogenarian named Helga Rathbone, an antique spinster with a history of suspicious behavior.

The county council claimed numerous people, who had rented rooms in her ancient mansion in the back hills outside of Elko, Nevada, had gone missing. Due to her low rent rate and our low income we decided to sign on for a year.

Our room, which resembled a small hut, contained among other things, her ancient upright piano. Judging by the proportion between the two, it appeared the piano came first and the room had been erected around it. Short of shoving it out the way-too-small window, the only hope to rid the room of it would be cutting the behemoth into firewood and feeding it to the giant maw of our chamber's wood stove. Quite certainly Helga would draw the line at such behavior, so we lived around the hulk.

Random overfed bookcases were clogged mostly with well worn mountain climbing books we used on adventures up granite walls. The remaining shelves ballooned with medical books, which Ashton worked frantically each evening to ignore.

In one corner, surrounded by a chaotic assortment of split logs and chunks of railroad-grade coal, hunched a massive relic of cast-iron in the form of a heating stove. The crusty firebox, nightly stoked to cherry red, fought bravely to fend off the icy snow-laden bite of winter's bitter fingers, while also serving as a drying rack for miscellaneous clothing and damp climbing gear. It also was a convenient (although forbidden) place to prepare a quick meal in a pan or a small pot.

A tall, wood bunkbed hovered safely across the room from the envious mouth of the stove. The bunk, which was sort of a home-away-from-home for Ashton, also housed a huge built-in desk, sagging slightly to the south and forever in the throws of vomiting forth its entire heaving collection. It included: a silent computer, remains of questionable meals, clean and dirty clothing, and books stuffed to overflowing with papers, and a scattered array of climbing gear, shooting equipment, and bicycle parts. A killing jar containing a gruesome assortment of miss-matched body parts, relics of some past biological study completed the still-life picture, and perching daringly on edge, anxiously ready to disgorge its contents into the mayhem.

Auspiciously hovering near the room's only window, was a large terrarium, forever daring to challenge the whims of gravity while balancing at a drunken tilt atop a well-stuffed and notably off-kilter bookcase. The terrarium was home to an overweight Black-Bearded Dragon, constantly on the prowl for live bait, while subtly feigning sleep or death. In an even darker quarter of the crowded room, asleep in a large kennel whose primary purpose was to abate a mound of questionably clean clothing from its emanate slide toward the floor, lurked a gangly black critter of questionable canine origin.

Most nights, and up to a point this one included, were no different one from another. On this particular night however, I arrived back from the mountains late and attempted an hour of writing in a solitude blessedly warmed by the red-faced monster in the corner. (Stove, not canine.) I gave up the battle to remain conscious and decided to retire to my down bag.

Taken with a last minute whim, I made a hasty journey down to the shadowy kitchen for something edible to devour with my nighttime cup of tea. Moving noiselessly, so as not to waken whatever lurked in those dark and closed walls, I poured tea into my mug, grabbed a banana and a questionable hunk of bread, and left rapidly, closing the kitchen door quietly behind me. Thus armed with food and the sloppy mug of hot sweet beverage, I stumbled back up darkened stairs already too asleep to attempt bed-time formalities and entered our chamber.

Still dressed against the cold and too sleepy to care, I crammed food into a slobbering mouth, gulped down the dregs of the rapidly cooling beverage and stuffed myself into the down sleeping bag, where I very shortly succumbed to exhaustion.

"Cozy slumber" may cross a less-informed mind at this point. Wrong, very wrong. Nothing "cozy" existed in our rented chamber, nor would I use "cozy" to describe any of the six other rented rooms, frequently silent and perhaps, empty, throughout the ancient structure which housed our *dungeon*.

My life changed in the next few shadowy hours, changed in manifestation both mentally and physically. I feel it is important to go back a couple of days to include you, the reader, in events leading up to this ghastly ordeal.

Prior to his departure on a climbing trip to Utah, Ashton left me food, instructions and the trust to tend to his pets: Wabish, the Dragon, and Ytlek, a half-breed wolfhound. I am ashamed to admit my own interests undermined his trust, and two days after he left I jumped ship and went up the mountain for a weekend of trekking on St. Mary's Pass.

What with being absent those days, arriving well after dark on the Sunday, and then forgetting to feed the critters upon return to our chamber, I had unknowingly added far too many hours to their involuntary fasting. In light of what transpired, it was my negligence overall which set into motion a most gruesome tragedy.

Feeding time

Dreams, fantasies, even nightmares. Oh yes, we've had them, had 'em all, and recovered nicely, thank you. In dreams you have time to think thoughts such as "Oh, how horrid," or "How lovely this all is." In dreamland you might just have enough time to escape the horror, to turn and walk away, perhaps embed yourself on a treadmill and run indefinitely as on an endless conveyor belt. In desperation, perhaps as a last resort, limbs trembling, stomach churning madly, brain on full retreat, you crawl; crawl as if in endless seething streams of treacle.

Shakespeare told us, perhaps warned us, *In dreams every wish rushes to a deed.*

That deed, maybe good, perhaps bad, often insane and criminal but no matter the suffering, the mind knows that "This is temporary; there is a release, the blessed release of awakening."

Dreams would have us suffer in fire, in snow, perhaps in ice; typically in agony. Yet through it all, we must trust waking up for the release from the angry debasement to reality, awake and return to the peace and calm of our chamber of slumber. All very fine if it works, but what if... just tolerate me here... what if the noise of screaming continues on and on and raises to a deafening crescendo, and the pain penetrates deeper and deeper into flesh and bone? Worse, if the mind realizes there is no release available and wakes to the terrible reality that...this, this is not a dream, and I am not asleep?

I slept fitfully that first hour or so. Slept because I was worn out from climbing, and slept because I realized that far too soon I had to be refreshed both mentally and physically, and be back at work again.

Time in the grave, time asleep, time unconscious; all are nonexistent. You go out and later on, except for death, come back around and have to check a clock to realize that five minutes or five hours have passed.

It was perhaps two hours later, when I surfaced slightly and realized I was twisted about in realms of roasting claustrophobic dementia within the frantic casting about of my overheated bag, resulting in a restraint of knots and dizziness. I progressed toward freedom as I became unwound from the sleeping bag and groped about in darkness for fresh airs of any temperature.

Standing stripped among the cold and dark, yet restored from the twisted garbs and bedding, I gripped the icy latch and wrenched open the heavy door. I stepped half out to greet the frantic wave of cold air hovering silently on the gloomy landing above the stairs.

Somewhat refreshed, I turned to gain the room and the comfort of my sleeping bag, when my eyes caught something moving within the dark chamber.

In the painfully slow seconds of hesitation, *it* had me! I was seized firmly by the legs, dragged back inside, and in a single blow to the head, went unconscious. I sensed rather than heard the second blow, as the door slammed against my escape. Dark as always, the chamber now became darkness obscured in black. Unconsciousness fell like the snows of late December.

The terror of blackness, of the unknown, of not knowing what, much less why, were all nothing against the agony of claws and teeth. These terrors from blackened nowhere, unseen yet felt and heard, were tending to their chores as they attacked again and again my frantically kicking legs.

"Ahh no, no, ahhhhh help, oh God help me!" The voice screamed on and on. Eventually I could identify it, and it was MY voice and it screamed endlessly. "Stop, stop, no! Oh help help! No, aaaaaaaaaah! Not more!"

No one heard. No one came. It went on and on.

Perhaps there were two of them judging from the amount of bites, and bone snapping crunches down on my legs. The attack came in a feeding frenzy and came again and again.

Bear. Maybe a coyote, but teeth, oh, angry teeth again and again. The blood flowed onto the floor and covered me, my shredded clothing, the disemboweled bag, blood everywhere. ...

Frantic scrambling, struggling, and gnashing of teeth, biting, clawing, the rough scrape of fur, of dry bristles, and the terrible crunch of bone. The swiping against my bloodied flesh of the scales of a reptilian creature, and biting, biting, biting,

At first fear, then struggling, a lifetime of seconds later, came terror. At the last I was craven, so craven.

I had the briefest of seconds to imagine Ashton's chagrin upon his arrival home.

"My room, oh no George, what, what's happened?" Then the realization slowly sinking into the core of reality.

"Dead, no! Oh no, not that. Not ...dead!"

Shaking now, a constant shaking and a voice speaking. Calling out and calling to someone named George.

"What in the world? Wake up man. Wake up! George, can you hear me? Stop the shouting, and wake up!"

Ashton?

"What the, where am I?" I reached out to grasp darkness, reached out in desperate hope, he took hold of my hand, and my mind; his presence waning the power my nightmare, a nightmare thankfully vanishing now.

"Ashton, you're here? Am I alive?" Stupid question really. I mean, I was sitting up, had tossed aside frantically twisted bedding, and finally stood up in the blackness, which was extinguished as he transformed a tiny match flame into the welcoming blaze of a lantern, and peered deeply into the gloom.

"Man, you were really out of it. You screamed on and on, and the things you said. Terrible stuff. Are you ok, now?"

I assured him that dreamland had spared me once more, and after the briefest of moments talk, Ashton, returned topside, and I crawled into a stressed and twisted sleeping bag. We both went under the spell of sleep as the night took over again.

I suspect I grinned as I slowly succumbed to the beckoning grasp of nature, as she pulled me deeper and deeper. I slept at last.

…then Ashton screamed, "My legs – oh no, my legs, someone help me!" Voice of a person in agony then, "Aaaaaaah, not biting, oh no, not that!"

It had started all over again!

SIN IN A SPRAY CAN

It was another Sunday. Just another "stuck indoors winter's day" in early December and I had decided to clean the utility room. Housed in that small crowded porch were the usual: washer and dryer, a bin of soiled clothing, three cats, their smelly litter box and …that darned storage cupboard. My plan included cleaning and organizing the cupboard and throwing away the accumulated junk gathered over the years.

I pulled open the cupboard doors and gazed at sagging shelves crammed full of jumbled small boxes, tins and spray bottles. The three cats were the first to get involved by pushing right into the floor-level space, initiating a landslide of overturned boxes, spilling laundry powder and a jumble of falling spray cans, all of which added fuel to the annoyance of the event. I stomped a heavy boot and two of the felines dived for their sleeping box while the smaller one, who could still fit, escaped to safety behind the dryer where only the snake-like 220 volt power cord could reach him.

The cleaning process began. I opened the back door to access the trash can and ushered in a cold nine o'clock morning and the hairy snout of my dog Astro, a huge Hungarian Shepherd. This initiated a further ruckus since the cats lived in terror of Astro, whose only wish was a short-lived cat chase. I politely asked him to leave because of course you don't *tell* a 150 pound dog to do anything.

Most of the tins, bottles and boxes were old, slightly damp and splitting at the seams. Soon, I had sorted out anything useful, and restocked the closet, while the remainder rested outside in the trash.

Finished with the hardest part, I set about sweeping the floor, when one last spray can felt inclined to roll out from a hiding place behind the cat box. It tinkled across the floor and stopped against my right foot, a bright red can with electric blue lettering.

I snatched it up and took aim at a lurking cat; fabric starch and cat fur could be such fun. The lettering stopped me short of the act; **Sin in a Spray Can** it read. *What the heck?*

The ridiculous article looked official but was obviously a joke and begged the question, "Who would have purchased this foolish item?"

Stupidity took over from common sense as I zipped off the plastic wrapper and removed the cap. I decided to give it a spray and see what was really in the can when the door into the kitchen opened and my nephew pushed into the confined space.

He tossed me a look of disbelief and asked, "What on earth are you doing so early on a Sunday?" When you're sixteen anything before eleven on Sunday is out of the question.

I showed him the spray can and laughed at his reaction. "It's a joke. Aim it at the cats and give it a shot."

Before I could react, he snatched the bottle, directed it at the unsuspecting cats and pressed the trigger.

Nothing.

He tried again.

Same thing.

At this point he shook it really hard, pointed it at his own face and said, "It's a stupid joke."

He squeezed the trigger one last time. *Zapp*, full in the face! He screamed, dropped the can, which rolled across the floor, emitting a slightly reddish fog, escaped into the kitchen and slammed the door.

Seconds passed. The can stopped fizzing. The cats and I looked puzzled. I had about decided it was all a joke, when from behind the closed kitchen door I heard frenzied shouts and the sound of dishes smashing, followed closely by the stomping of boots and terrified screams!

As I turned with a degree of self-survival reluctance to follow, I beheld the largest of the three cats, with horrifyingly monstrous talons fully extended, plunging them again and again into the face of its dying roommate, while the free-flowing blood began to cover the white-tiled floor. I was well aware of the normal reaction, but realized with a degree of shock that I was enjoying it!

Almost unconsciously I reached into the overhead cupboard and removed my hidden Colt 45. In an involuntary frenzy, I wrenched open the back door, fired once at the astonished Astro, and fled across the field toward a neighboring turkey farm.

Heck yeah. There are hundreds of them and turkeys are slow.

Bang! Bang!

Feathers flew and terrified shouts erupted from the farmhouse.

THOUGHTS OF A DYING SWIMMER

I went overboard, about three o'clock on a warm July afternoon. But like they say, *Jockeys* don't fall off of their horses, they are thrown off, and *Sailors* don't fall off their boats, rather they are pushed off. In my case, the boom swung over and swiped me overboard. Semantics aside, I was dumped into cool Pacific Ocean waters about four miles from the nearest shore, and was thoroughly unprepared for it.

On that lazy day's sail from Santa Catalina to Santa Barbara onboard the *Sri Lanka*, my Coronado 24, I was doing what you do on a lazy day: sipping some cool Hawaiian pineapple juice, enjoying some sunshine while wearing a Speedo and a Skim Line harness; the Speedo in order to gain the most suntan possible. (Vanity was never an issue with me.) The harness was standard issue, designed to attach me to my boat should I go overboard, an event no sailor ever plans on but must prepare for. In any event I had failed to attach the safety line from the boat to the harness because what the heck, I was not planning to leave the boat mid-ocean.

The airs that day were light, and I was beating close to the wind when I stood up to adjust some rigging. One could not have guessed, on that warm July afternoon, that it was I who was destined to become the next victim of the hungry blue Pacific Ocean.

The boom swung across just about the time I stood up to make the adjustment and…as I hit the cool water I had the chance to think, *Crap, I'm not hooked to the boat; grab that stern line!*

Typically onboard small sailboats, you stream a line about five meters long off the stern for just that reason, something to grab on to and pull yourself back onto the boat. On the end of the line you tie a large knot, called a Monkeys Fist, so the line does not just slide through your hands and leave you, watching your boat sail away.

Following the initial cold shock and the typical gulp of unwanted salt water, I surfaced sputtering and slightly disoriented, made a grab for the line and felt it slide through my shaking hands. I had failed to tie the knot; and in stark horror I looked up to see my blue and white Coronado unknowingly leave me behind.

Most days I arrive at the lap pool before 4 a.m. so I can get in my 1.5 mile swim early. It's something I do weekdays as regularly as I eat, sleep and work. It's what makes me a fairly good and tireless swimmer. That's what entered my mind as the lifeline left my hands that day. *You're a swimmer, go for it.*

I pounded through the face-slapping waves, far less forgiving than any lap pool, for a good five minutes before I realized I needed more power. My arms and legs were not doing it, and I wasn't gaining on my boat. I was losing that day's race, which unlike my calm, somewhat heated, morning workout, was held in cold salt water, unevenly tossed about with waves and irregular current, tides and unpredictable sea life. With a resentful degree of submission, I relaxed and watched the *Sri Lanka* begin to move off into a lazy summer's afternoon.

And I swam on.

When you sail, there are a few rules for survival if you intend to harmonize with the ocean's power and arrive at your destination. You need to be familiar with: wind speed and direction, sea current, navigation, weather outlook, and in case you are stupid enough to end up in the water, add to the list water temperature and sea life. So I swam on, watching the stern lettering on my vessel move ahead of me, hopefully toward our destination of Santa Barbara. I'd hate to lose that boat, but it would appear that she was going to reach our destination first.

And I swam on.

I began to take account. I was not dressed to endure cold ocean water for very long. Even with the constant calories generated and lost, both in swimming and shivering, my skinny frame was eventually going to become cold, and my suntan was not going to do a thing to keep me warm. In my favor was the fact that I could pause between bouts of strokes, my slight harness was in fact designed to be somewhat buoyant and would allow me to rest and float.

Rescue? Hmmmm, now let's see. Who was going to come to my aid? Well, not my landlady; she was pretty much a stay-at-home smoker, who lived for the daytime television shows and a weekly visit from the milkman. Maybe my girlfriend? Nope, she had dumped me for someone who owned a Mercedes Benz and offered vastly more fun than time spent onboard a sailboat on a cold, miserable, seasick, hungry day in the ocean. That left a few sailing friends, mostly who had families to entertain, and none of whom were aware that I had run off once again to visit nearby islands while choosing a solo crossing. Nope, what I had to rely on was a 6 foot 1 inch tall frame, 140 pounds of skin, bone, muscle and bleached blond hair; OK, plus a red and white speedo, and a red harness.

And I swam on.

Ahead was a slightly choppy sea, a white glare from an afternoon sky, the stern of the *Sri Lanka,* an indication of some land form and thoughts, thoughts, thoughts. I could keep myself occupied and in good company day and night with all that my vivid imagination had in store.

I was a writer, and the very thought of something new or different proffered up all forms of wild notions. I kept myself busy with technical thoughts: thoughts of friends and my family, thoughts of boats and cars and fickle girlfriends, and kept myself busy with thoughts of anything except the thing I fought to not think about - sharks.

Don't think about sharks! I talked to myself, thought to myself, raged against the thoughts. I tried to not think about sharks. It failed to work. And as hard as I lectured to my mind, *Remember to forget such thoughts,* I failed and my stupid mind thought about - Sharks.

I am certain that the ocean is occupied with worse things than sharks.

Let's see, I instructed myself as I watched the *Sri Lanka* aim her bow toward a spot on the coast, slightly north of where I placed my early on destination of Santa Barbara.

There are giant, man-eating whales, huge, biting octopuses, jellyfish with long, stinging tails, sting rays with ditto, scorpion fish, and stonefish and, well, the list is endless.

Heck I'm a swimmer, surfer and a sailor; I'm not an oceanographer, or whatever they're called. I left that to a science teacher in my first year of college, whom l never liked, in a class I liked even less. But for an absolutely stunning Asian girl in the second row behind me, well heck I would have dropped that class. As it was; well eventually we went out. Enough of that.

So Michael, stop worrying about sharks and worry about all the other stuff that might kill you! Great, now I'm going to worry all the more! That little pep-talk didn't help one bit. I continued to worry about monsters from the deep, currents and tides, the fact that I was getting colder and where was I actually headed.

And I swam on.

I alternated between breast stroke and crawl stroke, exactly what I did each morning in the pool.

What I did? Now I had to ask myself, *Is that all over with? Are you going to die here and never get to play the silly morning swimming game with Joanne and Bill again?*

Now I had something else to worry about, and that made a huge list. I got busy worrying and didn't concentrate so much on exactly where I was headed or which stroke I was using.

And I swam on.

I was suddenly aware of a noise, a sort of droning noise, a throbbing, slightly underwater noise.

Submarine!

I had been on submarines in the Navy. Now wouldn't that be ironic if I was rescued by a submarine? More so if it happened to be one on which I had been stationed. Then I remembered, one of them was in a U.S. Navy museum at Pearl Harbor. Another one was so old it had been cut up to make razor blades, or something. And the third one? Now I started to cry, and must have made the already salty ocean even more salient. That third submarine had been lost with all hands, about three years after I had been stationed onboard. I cried often when I thought of those men; a few of whom I had known, and all who had to endure so incomprehensible a death with nothing to do about it but die.

Shut up, stupid. Damn it, just shut up!

I blew up then, and went into a rage with nothing but the ocean waves to vent on. I thrashed about, screamed, lost control, and gulped blasted, sticky salt water, and cried all the more.

And then I remembered God!

And, since He is not one to push back, I went ahead and screamed and yelled and swore at Him.

"It's your fault! You could save me! You could have given me someone to sail with so that I would not be alone! You took away my wife and now no one loves me enough to spend time with me."

There, now I had it. I could blame God for this unfortunate accident, and scrape all the other pieces of life's hardships into his lap at the same time.

"Why don't you love me enough to even care?"

I went on shouting and screaming until I slowly realized that it is only because of His immeasurable and unending love that I, or any of us, am alive and have the hope of life and eternity. Gradually I resumed some control.

And I swam on.

Relentlessly, the noise droned on, and I had a sudden vision of the outsides of a submarine right below the mid-ship line. There, on the waist, three quarters of the way back from the bow, was the deep water-intake pump covered with an iron grating! The massive grid of iron was designed to allow water to be sucked in to cool engine systems but would not allow objects, such as floating debris, or stupid scared swimmers, to be drawn in. All well, except when you are sucked up against the deep sea chest you will remain there until the vessel surfaces and you float free or you're pulled off…dead! Something new to worry about; something more to add to the list.

And I swam on.

Something touched my leg and instantly I knew it was that deadly shark, whose teeth were busily tearing suntanned skin away from my skinny muscles and bones. I refused to peer down eye-to-eye with that beast which would be my finish.

"Go ahead stupid, take a look!"

I looked. The monster was a plastic jug half full of seawater and *100% Organic Apple Juice*. I actually was so terrified I vomited into the already polluted ocean, adding what was left of my last meal to whatever else floated around the area. At that very moment the waves seemed much calmer, so the nasty mess stayed with me forever. Sooner or later I left it far behind,

As I swam on.

I gradually realized three things: I had become colder without being aware of it, I had lost my direction, and it was getting darker. A new worry! I would never see my way to shore in the darkness and *it* would never see me in the dark before it hit me.

"How far? How bloody far must I swim?"

I forged ahead, through darkening waters and unknown *sea monsters*. I crawl-stroked myself half way around the world that night, and wound up still swimming.

Where, I mean, where in the world am I?

No street signs in the ocean, just waves and waves and waves.

And I swam on.

Ahead of me, not off to one side, not miles off but almost directly ahead of me were lights! These lights shouted *shore, safety* and *help at hand*. I was cautious with tentative hope. After all, why get my hopes up just to drown miles off course when I thought I was headed into a peacefully comforting, warm and safe marina with cascades of food and drink, hot water baths and people to provide me with hope and security. I headed for those dockside lights and the uncertain hope they proffered up to all those tired swimmers just in from Santa Catalina Island.

And I swam on.

I swam on toward security and hope, only to be condemned to death by a voice which shouted, "Shark! Shark! Mike watch out, it's a shark!" The shouting went on and on. "Shark, shark!"

The fact that someone out in the wild, blue Pacific knew my name never posed any particular bewilderment; I didn't want a shark and I refused to look around. Instead, I focused on those lights way up ahead, lights most courteously offering hope and security, glowing from some dockside port, some foreign safe harbor onshore the edge of the blue and menacing Pacific. A Pacific Ocean of salt-bath infested waters of despair and certain doom.

"Shark, shark. Mike, get out of the water! Blood attracts sharks!"

I didn't need telling of that gruesome fact; I was aware that a crimson blush to the water served to give any roaming evening shark the late-night munchies.

The voice was female and slightly calming too. What did it mean to an exhausted, frightened, bone-chilled swimmer to hear a female voice shouting the death chant over the darkened Pacific coast waters?

"Shark Mike! Shark! Come on, Mike, and climb out. You're bleeding from a cut foot. Get out or you'll attract a cruising man-eating machine."

What was going on? I stopped swimming and touched down on firm footing, on smooth tile and cement, in shallow water. I glanced about at soft lighting, at a warm atmosphere, into the eyes of Joanne and Bill, poolside at my morning swim club.

"What on earth? Where am I?" I was confused to the point of insanity.

"Mike." It was Bill with his reassuring, coach-like voice. "Mike, you cut your foot on a bad flip-turn back at the other end of the pool; you're bleeding."

He grinned and continued. "You'll turn the waters crimson and attract a prowling shark. We saved you from a certain early morning death." He offered me a hand as I hopped out of the pool and was handed a warm, dry towel to swath my foot in.

"Shark? But why all the shark scare?" I was relieved, but a little angry too.

"Heck man, we had to do something to get your attention and 'shark attack' just came to mind." He grinned and the two of them wandered off to do morning chores.

Still slightly dazed, I limped into the locker room to shower and dress for work.

I didn't want to be late for my job at the aquarium, feeding the sharks.

I did, in fact swim that distance to shore that day, reached the far off Santa Barbara Marina and the safety of dockside lights. I did see, not so far ahead the stern of my Coronado, tied to a mooring at the public docks. As I swam those last yards, climbed a ladder and flopped onto comforting wood dock planks, I was not at first welcomed by loving ladies and friendly dockside workers who were on hand to take into their care exhausted swimmers from far out at sea.

"Hey, you! You can't lie about these public docks like that." An angry voice of a dockside worker with a dirty wrinkled uniform and a mouth to match.

"This aren't no sun bathing beach for vagrants, move on and get off of here."

Oh crap, a merchant marine officer disguised as a slovenly dock-side worker with a mile long ego and a whip for a tongue. "Sir, I fell overboard out at sea. I just swam halfway here from Santa Catalina Island and I'm exhausted and freezing cold."

I gazed about. "And there," pointing a shaking slightly wrinkled hand, "There is my boat, *Sri Lanka*, my own boat. It arrived safely here just ahead of me."

I thought of the little stateroom below deck and of warm dry clothing and a down sleeping bag, and at once staggered onto stumbling feet and crabbed my way toward my craft.

The want-to-be marine officer was faster. "Oh no you don't; that's someone's boat safely berthed here for them, not for some half naked nut-case from the homeless beaches of our coastal sanctuary."

He made as if to toss me back into the cold dark seawater when…

"Hey, hold on there! That man owns that boat and has anchored it here off and on over the past year." My friend Dick appeared from *The Sea Cup*, a slightly below grade B watering hole for sailors, tourists, and tonight a sanctuary for cold, wrinkled swimmers fresh in from the salty Pacific.

Dick and I retired to my cabin for warm, dry clothing, then into the pub for a hot grog and sandwich. He listened to my story between quaffs of his mug of powerful black ale and embellished it with hilarity and shaking of a bleached head of hair with beard to match.

I overnighted in a warm beachfront hotel costing a month's boat payment, well worth every penny, with a deep hot tub of soapy water and a warm bed to sink into. Morning took me to a breakfast spot for coffee, eggs, and toast before I sailed my blue and white craft back to my rented mooring at the Ventura Marina.

I tied a monkey's fist to my stern line, invested in a more substantial harness, which included an emergency strobe light for those *night time* swims and continued to sail, mostly alone, all over the coastal waters off Southern California.

And I swam on.

J1951

I tossed the first body-sized bag into the furnace at about 0200. Flames gushed from cracks in the burn box, encroaching smoke strangled the urge to breathe and vicious heat drove me back against the steel bulkhead. While the horrors of a shipboard fire raged through my mind, the logic of logistics reminded me that we were on land.

The metal of the door was double half inch rolled steel; made to withstand storms, fire and bullets. Time, hard use and harsh weather conditions year-round had tested the first two, while oxidation had peppered fractions of the surface with tiny needle-sized holes allowing frantic jets of daylight inside for a look about. The iron compartment was only occupied at night; little notice was granted to invading shafts of light.

The unwieldly door, hanging on hulking steel hinges, gave way to a confined steel room. Almost the entire space was filled with one colossal oil-fired furnace. Incinerator and crew had a single impatient function, to cremate selected items and reduce them to ash, dead ash. That job required very little space.

The smell behind the metal door was greasy and stirred up horrible images of a charnel house. With a guarded eye, I looked about for a collection of long boxes. Old, sticky and sooty gray finish everywhere assured me this was in fact a place to incinerate unwanted things; dead bodies came to mind. Hours after the burning tank had cooled, overpoweringly pungent dead ash still filled the air.

"In you go now, lock up and give us the code when you want out; unless of course you intend to spend the whole night inside!"

The guards outside the burning room slammed the heavy steel door to, threw the outside lock tight and waited for us to do the same. *Clank!* The door locked from without and within; double secure. Who would care, who would come and would want to enter anyway?

We were U.S. Navy *snoops* and manned an intercept facility, a remote naval communications station atop the *Hill* on the island of Adak. Situated at the southwestern tip of the Aleutian Islands, we lived year round in winter's harsh grip. Snow, ice, wind, and frozen flattened tundra matted beneath her bleakness. It was said the elements of winter had their origin on the island of Adak. We believed it.

We were communication technicians, part of an exclusive branch of the Naval Communications Department. Daily or nightly, depending on our duty shift, as we entered the locked-radio spaces we came to call home, we were chillingly reminded by a brass plaque on the bulkhead, just how vulnerable and expendable we were.

The icy-ironic words of the plaque spelled it out in cryptic sardonicism:

> *"In the event of an island invasion:*
> *Tower guards will detonate explosives to flood the runway,*
> *Watch officers will ignite charges on all communications equipment,*
> *Marine guards will shoot the CTs."*

We were the CT's, the communication technicians, the *snoops*. Our future, in the event of invasion loomed dark and conclusively final.

The brown burn sacks, destined for the hungry flames of the furnace, arrived nightly from up the hill; arrived under armed marine guard. Men were selected from the mid watch (2400 to 0800) to "burn" these sacks. We were typically nabbed from our sleepy radio positions between 0200 and 0400, some of the least active times of communications.

The bulging brown burn sacks contained a feast of information, a wealth of clues, and clear proof that we knew what they knew, also where and when we had collected it. Those bags, the remains of communications traffic intercepted and transcribed, were guarded and destroyed at all cost.

"Shoot the CT's," because "Dead men tell no tales."

With the oil feed fully open and the fire complaining loudly we would feed the patient sacks into the maw of the oven; feed them one sack at a time.

Some of us had dour rituals for this job; no single one lent a degree of self-respect to our "military" characters.

"Here you go Lars, toss in the next body, more fodder for the flames."

Such comments spoke sadly of our attitude at the time. The mind, bored by the nightly drudgery replayed sad moments from history to cover emotions otherwise hidden within. We had to be certain that each bag was completely incinerated before feeding in the next bag.

"Stir those ashes, you there, you there, don't standby idly about. Stir those ashes, and make certain no evidence remains." We made certain too. Each bag must disappear completely; only a fine powder would remain after each burn, and it was eventually bagged and taken aloft in a Coast Guard PBY and scattered over mute and icy Bearing Sea waters.

My burn partner one night was a callous 2nd class named Bandage. He wasted no time voicing his attitude toward that depressing episode long past, long past and best forgotten, yet frequently in thoughtless light-hearted jest most painfully rehearsed.

Lars, (His name for me since my name of Eric von Heinrich, although Dutch, sounded German to him.) "*Lars,* how many did you cremate in the Holocaust days, eh?"

"Let's just do the job and not discuss such stupid notions. I'm nineteen years old, far too young to have lived during that war."

My father, however, had lived in Germany, had been swallowed up by the Holocaust and had perished. Evacuated just in time, the rest of our family had survived. I still held dear his memory, his face dances before me in dreams.

Images linger in my mind of the inevitable horrid news that his decomposed body, still bearing the tattooed number *J1951,* had been recovered from a stinking-open pit on the grounds of Auschwitz.

I despised the simple-mindedness of those who only half understood, who realized no loss from that bleak time in history. Bandage considered himself funny while actually wearing nicely the cloak of an anti-intellectual dullard.

"Here you go *Lars,* toss in another body, another Steiner, another Goldberg. Hey, did your whole family participate, huh? Did they each take a turn at the hearth-side?"

I was entirely too tired of his stupid insults that night. Any notion that I would be part of the machine which destroyed my father was just too much.

"Rot you Bandage, you stupid boor. Shut up that dirty hole in your face and just do your job. Just shut up about my family."

Now I had touched a nerve. Bandage grew redder, if possible. His face growing uglier, with fleshy globs for pale, pulpy cheeks, a flap of dirty red hair, a mouth crammed with crooked tobacco-stained teeth, all of which leered at me in the uncaring heat of the burn box.

My job up the hill suffered as my mind was ablaze with the fire and ashes of the burn building. I was fascinated, mesmerized, held in the grips of that burn shed. Days past when I did not venture far from that blackened shop of terror; it was part of me, carved into my mind, controlling my thoughts. Nightly, as I stood my watch, I waited with lust and terror for the order to, "Hold the burn."

And then one night, "How did you feel as they slid off the table into the fire?"

Bastard!

"Did you grin and laugh? How about cringe and shiver, or perhaps just have a 'Get on with the job' attitude? Huh *Lars?* How did you feel as the bodies crackled and popped and went all wrinkled and smoky?"

In blind fury I lunged at him then, shoving the ugly, insulting monster against the red hot wall of the oven; pressing him tight, tight enough to smell his pants scorching when I screamed my anger into his panicky face.

"You filthy rat. How dare you accuse me, you stinking pig, you swine!" I gasped for words. "You are as bad as those you accuse, worse perhaps."

In emotions of frenzied heat, challenging the very oven as I grew hotter by the second, I grappled with him. One lunge and his grotesque face hovered near the white heat of the huge oven, and then, in crazed passion I shoved the final few inches.

"Ahh no, oh God no! Ahh *Lars*, no, aaaaah!" He screamed and screamed and screamed; but softer then, rage and insults simmering slowly into frantic whimpers, then the wilting mouth fell silently dead.

No one would know, no one would open the door without the code, and now I alone had that code. Bandage had taken his with him to a dark place where doors remained locked forever.

"Take your stupid name calling, your prejudice and your illness toward mankind. Take those and all your rotten insults and take them to hell!"

I screamed at his face, at the appalling roasted splotchy mess he had become, and at the raging storm inside and out.

I screamed for all those who had died mute with no chance to scream for themselves. I screamed for a father, for a dad, loved and lost. I screamed for that one man among three million dumped mute into an odorous pit of equally nondescript and passionlessly silent bodies. I fell against his lifeless body and screamed for J1951.

I had to dispose of the body quickly as the guards would want that door opened soon and want to know why my job was only partly completed. There were no further body bags to burn, only the one left mangled against the smoking-hot oven, dead but still conspicuous.

I pressed down the foot lever and the huge iron fire box door slid up, exposing leaping hungry flames within.

I struggled with the ugly dead body, detested the closeness of the face to mine, as I slung it over my arms and dumped it into the ravenous oven. The final shove left only an arm sticking out, just one arm, the left arm, wanting a finishing shove in and with that gesture, the evidence was banished and the job was completed.

I gripped the flesh and fabric and attempted to tug it into place, Smoking cloth fell away as did roasted flesh, exposing only a portion of the forearm just by the elbow. And as I twisted and maneuvered that final evidence of my night's chore into the fire the letters fell into my view.

"What?" Did I see…but of course it could not have been…*J1951*!

I crushed the door down, and hammering home the latch for the final time, completed my night's duty and alerted the sleepy guards outside. With a rasping grown of disgruntlement the reluctantly rusty outer door opened slowly.

In a shaken and tormented state I was free, free to be released back to my cold dismal hut.

The code rapped out into the icy night's air, allowed that the freezing guards in the depressing outer expanse could release me to my situation in an equally cold and dismal hut.

"So, A1140, I see you have finished the burn. Very good; you have done well and can return to your hut. You will be back again however, just remember. You will return."

The road back was long and stretched ahead into a depressing snow-blown night. In dread-anticipation I shuffled along in the stilled darkness, one with the cold bleak four am gloom and the lonely crawl up the dreaded roadway toward those damning gates:

'Arbeit Macht Frei.'

I trudged along and looked up at ice-shrouded nodding heads of silently indifferent railroad lamps. Those tired, dim lights cast their feeble rays down to my path, to my feet, and offered little both of light and of hope to my utterly mortified state.

I entered the gates, walked to my hut and joined the countless other branded, layered and imprisoned.

The next day they called for A1140 and then it was my turn to be pushed inside, but not to burn, rather to be burned.

And then I too vanished, vanished into the hot darkness of obscurity, vanished to join the other silent millions.

If there is any way to recognize, to remember, to honor the sad
state of all those who perished at the hands of the Nazi War
Machine, then this feeble attempt at a recognition of them is meant
to respect, to honor, to remember them each one. In no way is
this meant to mock or belittle the situation of those individuals
in that far past, yet not to be forgotten time of history.

THE TENTH FRAME

I hadn't truly looked at the pictures on the walls before. I mean after all, the rooms were dark, drafty, massive and cluttered with heavy dark furniture, therefore, when I eventually had a chance to sit a spell and enjoy the large fire I had built, I was instantly taken with the reality of the framed visages immortalized on those dark-plank walls.

They were all older style photos, head shots and some profiles, and yet each one – well, each photo came to life in its own bleak and somber manner. I was astonished to sense a likeness to persons well known in history. There was a man almost a twin to Teddy Roosevelt. Another looked like Sir Winston Churchill. Further along I discovered William Shakespeare, and over there was former President George Washington. Napoleon was across the darkened hallway holding a private Waterloo, and alone, by the entry hung Henry VIII with no wives to lend comfort.

How fitting. Further along and last on the list, was an empty frame. Perhaps some photo had fallen out and became lost. I glanced about but saw nothing. An empty frame in the midst of such company seemed a lost soul and I was tempted to remove it. I stopped then, realizing that, after all why should I recognize these people; I had never met them and I was almost certain they had never visited this drafty old lodge owned by my cousin Noel. I must be tired, hallucinating. Why, I even saw one photo that reminded me very much of Noel himself. Odd. Why would he have his own photo on the walls with these strangers? Well, it could be someone else too. It had been ages since I had actually visited or even seen Noel.

Curiosity pulled me around the place, my eyes rambled. There was much to attract one's gaze in the room: large furniture, the massive beamed ceiling, long-dark drapes on impressive French windows, lots of diamond glass and British plank and beam walls. That sort of thing tended to pull the eye a bit. It was an effort to locate those 8 x 10 framed photos mounted on these walls of ancient oak, walls weathered by smoke and oil beneath a gentle patina of age and grandeur. They gave benediction to sometime past, as does an elderly lady at a gathering lend substance to what youth can never overcoat in its flash and flurry.

So I wandered the room, sipping my mug of hot tea and letting my eyes gaze upon the heads affixed to those walls in flat-black wood boxes. I stopped before the individual faces again. I was drawn to their sober and guarded gazes. I sensed that the hand of time had granted them each far more than half a century of age. Why, as I visited them did they seem to turn from me and appear to harvest age as a fall windstorm gathers its burden of leaves?

Now bear with me, what I am going to relate taxes one. For a fact, I will never grow accustomed to what happened during those days; those cold, remote, best-forgotten mid-December days in Northumberland, England.

For what seemed ages, I had been invited by my distant cousin Noel, to spend a weekend at his estate outside of Erlington; an invitation I had put off so often I was ashamed to call or even write. Time and distance considered, we were not close, yet we were now the last of cousins in the family. In my strongbox rested a will for what I had amassed during 52 years. Those listed items, some worth and some perhaps worthless were to be vested into the possession of young Noel at my passing.

Wishing a return to the peaceful post-war soils of England, I had flown over from my home in Maine, U.S.A. for a few months of a working holiday. My research into architectural history took me to the north of England and indeed to the rooms I rented in Farnsworth.

I had taken a cold day-lighter down from Farnsworth to a small station in East Ely. From there I had hired a car, an elderly canvas- topped Humber, to drive the 68 kilometers east to his noble, if aged home.

Actually, Noel had not called me in person this time, rather his barrister had rung up my office on Commerce Street, where I kept a solitary room for my drafting and writing. It seemed Noel wanted some drains redirected on the old estate and needed a bit of a survey run, and his secretary questioned whether I might consider driving around for the weekend.

With one thing and another, I was not away until the last train of the Friday and driving slowly in the unfamiliar countryside, I arrived later in the evening than I had first expected. I doubt that he even got the message; rather I suspect he gave up waiting, gathered up his tramping kit and vanished into the foggy and damp countryside for a hiking holiday into the uplands.

I struck out. However, I knew the location of his latchkey keeper and went around to her cottage. She was most willing to let me into his great stone lodge known as *The Shutters*, and even showed me the larder, woodbox, ale locker and where Noel kept his shotgun. The latter, for what enemies I had not a clue, save perhaps the odd castle ghost on a rampage. I digress.

So I built up a great log fire and sat near its comfort with a hot rum punch, to relax and warm up some rather chilled bones. Only then was I able to actually take in the full effect of the ten framed and glassed specters there gathered. They seemed to hold a certain command over the room's deeper reaches of moody climate and gloom. Had it not been a bleak, cold night, perhaps sunlight slanting in through the massive windows would do something to flourish relief to dinginess and shadows. The faces, stern, yet open too, looked out at the room with astonishment and awe. They hung in rapt respect for the dark unknown and displayed a hint of fear. I found myself looking over my shoulder into gloom and flicker of firelight. I arose and switched on soft pale reading lamps, thereby adding dark-dancing shadows to the chill and bleakness which the night therein harbored.

Two of the framed somber-faced specters guarded the door into the scullery. I passed them on my way in and out to renew my drink and eventually to cut a couple of thick meat and cheese sandwiches. The *door guards* almost gained a censure-like stance as I entered their domain. The one on the left was old and gloomy, the other somewhat stern and military.

Upon the third trip out form the scullery, I stopped in astonishment with mouth agape. The elderly gentleman had somehow slumped downward into the corner of the frame! I guess I had just not looked closely enough to realize just how far gone he was; wrinkled, dried-up and gaunt.

A quick look to the right lent a new meaning to aghast. There was something happening here that was most disquieting. There was that same stern continence, same military look, same hawk beak too. However, there was more. Now the man did indeed wear a military uniform, perhaps German from World War I; also an officer's hat, no doubt about that. The obvious question was, why was this all new and strange? Had he not worn those same clothes just minutes before? People don't switch garments within a photo frame. People do not age either, and yet my man on the left was a certain fifteen to twenty-five years older than when I viewed him on previous passages to the scullery. Perhaps it would be best if I just stopped parading back and forth before they both die of old age.

I dropped into a chair, a much used and massaged dark-leather maroon-colored chair; sat mentally exhausted and languished by the fire a bit to speculate on my vivid imagination. I suspect I dozed for several comfortable minutes prior to waking with a jerk.

The noise which upset my slumber appeared to be the old gent and his frame falling from the wall to the floor! I got up and looked for broken glass and such, but found only the wood frame. When I prepared to rehang it in its place, I realized something odd indeed. The photo was blank! No old man, no wizened wretch shrunken into the corner. Nothing remained. The best I would do was stare and ponder over the strange things we must encounter in later years.

That other photo, the one of the military officer, was holding silent sway at the door to the scullery. The officer was looking gray and tired. Perhaps he too was worried about his missing friend. I hoped I could find the lost photo on the floor, however, following a brief look into darkened corners, he and his picture frame, had joined the missing persons list. Was I at fault? I felt responsible, since I was alone in the house.

In time, I grew tired and realized it was almost midnight. I chose to sleep on the sofa near the fire. It was comfortable and the fire offered a warm companionship. I also privately thought it very certainly would not be tranquil spending a night alone upstairs, in one of those dark rooms.

I elected the friendship of the remaining faces on the wall. I walked over to Mr. Churchill. He was not having one of his best days. His cigar had burnt all but his lips, his eyes squinted well below half mast, his Homburg was slouched lower than usual and worry had painted a haggard look on his countenance. *"This was our finest hour,"* and well that comment may have applied to some point in time, however I suspected this was not one of them.

I turned and walked to the hall to locate a closet with blankets, and upon returning to the sofa to lay out my night's bed, I distinctly heard a gasp from the door into the scullery. I turned in start, my eyes grasped the corner of the captain's photo as it danced off the wall and slapped the floor in a most unmilitary manner. I reached for it among the shadowy floorboards and rehung the undamaged frame. His photo, however, was also missing!

The trip into the scullery would never be the same. I was sure that photos was also on the floor someplace.

I glanced up at the next face in the array about the room and looked into a very perplexed and aged Teddy Roosevelt. He had perhaps been beating his horse up San Juan Hill far too often, or perhaps the horse had beaten him up. Either way, the moniker of every kid's *"Teddy Bear"* was down in the mouth and down in the corner of the frame also.

It was too dark, I was too tired, and it was far too perplexing a situation to deal with that night. I retired, along with the eight survivors in their respective places along the cold and bleak walls of *The Shutters*.

The solemn, soft, death-like silence in that room would have been enough to make anyone drift off to a deep and comfortable sleep. I did my best to *drift off* and failed. It was with all of my efforts that I reacted to the night as such. I struggled to remain awake, fought the slide into restfulness, beat back the arm of calm and peace.

Dylan Thomas penned, *"Do not go gentle into that good night..."* Believe me, I held out and, *"Raged against the dying of the light."* I suspect my fellows on those bleak walls did the same. My mind refused to allow me that trip over the edge into a zone we all know so well, "...*for the dead know nothing...*"

As we sleep, time tends to gather her bounty from our remaining life: it will race down rails of iced glass, grind uphill on steps of granite and fend off the forever unwelcomed "*Dawn's early light.*" We can sleep for five minutes and awaken fresh as from a full night of it. We can also crawl out after nine hours of solitude and still feel drained and weary. Thus went my first night in *The Shutters* which would remain "*A night to remember.*"

I surfaced at about two am and padded about in stocking feet to build up the dying embers and embrace a mug of hot tea. I felt sort of bashed, and realized I had eaten very little and had failed to brush my teeth; a fact which was of itself not a great crime at my age. However, my mouth felt something akin to the inside of a fireman's glove in June. I visited the bath to refresh. On the way to the hall. my gaze fell again upon Teddy Roosevelt. He had taken a stance, no more of a squat, in the far corner of the frame. His face outlasted any job nature did to ancient weathered oak trees. His eyes sagged toward earth and gravity had taken its toll on the once proud lip which had emitted that celebrated cry, "*Charge the blockhouse,*" and swept it into a slurry of flab and wrinkles. I suspected he was not going to be with us for long.

Upon my journey into the bath I gazed into the mirror. "No! Not that!" I took a third look and, badly shaken, made my way out to the fireside. The night light and my somewhat turbulent state had left me feeling aged beyond my fifty-two years. The visage in the mirror told me all that I must face, we age exponentially under conditions of shock. The night at *The Shutters* had all the nurturing of an incubator. I looked ninety!

In my journey to the scullery I made another thick sandwich and a further cup of hot tea with honey, and with a refilled stomach and warmer body, I crawled back beneath the comforter and gazed into the fire. No overt gaze, no casual sentinel from the gallery of eight spoke out to assuage my agony at discovering my physical state that hour. No idyllic voice quieting my fearful and traumatized state. I was on my own. Body apart from self, I was stuck in a time and place I would rather never have visited.

I slept fitfully, and at five am, as cows were being milked in dairies across the country, the late Teddy Roosevelt dropped to the floor from the still dark ramparts of my chamber. I sensed it almost more than heard it. I realized something was wrong on that side of the room. A clean sweep of the walls told my eyes all that my ears had not relayed, Teddy was on the floor, and most likely, lost. I did not jump up to render help. He had gone to a place where I was not yet welcome.

Following another sleepless hour I was up for the day. The act of searching for Teddy failed to produce more than one dead mouse, some dust and of course the empty frame. I replaced it on the worn spot against the far wall. He was now only a memory. Perhaps in time the name would replace the vision. For now he was still the late Mr. President Theodore A. Roosevelt.

I was certain that in the dawn's early light I could make out what exactly was at hand. I was sure that all those remaining photos, along with those lost, and all the astonishing noises in the dark were just part of the night. In the light of day it would be different. I was right. It was different; it was vastly worse!

For starters, there was no fresh sun-filled solarium to waken me to a warm and cheery breakfast. The long dark night had vanished into a bleak, freezing-wet storm front. The darkness of day was just a little lighter darkness. It was also wetter, colder, and remarkably even more blustery. It was a dawn filled with the cataclysmic crashes and phosphoric flashes of nature gone mad. She had produced a massive electrical storm. Outside, nature worked her marvelous hand in a painterly approach to wreak havoc and tumult.

Secondly, there was no lovely gathered family to sit with and break the fast. I was alone in a monolithic wilderness occupied by a small group (growing smaller by the hour) of has-been look-alikes engaged in some fanciful race toward cessation and the long box. I made up my mind right then to deal with the situation as a battle front; I was angry. This must stop, and I was going to come to grips with it. First thing on the plan was for something to eat, then a warmer fire, and lastly a look around outside for an escape plan, in case all else failed.

In the scullery I faced a cold and clammy larder filled with rather elderly odds and ends, none of which made my mouth water; rather they turned my stomach. I put together a shepherd's pie, cut a piece of questionable bread from a rapidly-aging loaf, and brewed up another cup of steaming tea. Rather than chance the chills of that dank space I returned to the warmer fireside for my meal.

I hastily built up the fire with logs from the ample woodbin. The trip among the zone of those missing in action brought me up short. I realized something bold was underway across the room. An adventure into the unknown brought me face to face with a very gaunt yet bloated "Winnie," the Prime Minister, Sir Winston Churchill. He was hunkered over an old ledger, perhaps still at his studies to improve that forever elusive reading skill. Call it by any other name, he was on the day's docket for obsequy, and soon I feared.

Back across the room it was hard to tell what had happened. The remains of a fine early American hung in tatters against the newel post at the stair. Mr. President, George Washington, needed to be seen in hospital and soon I would judge, according to his condition. Instead, I was only able to give his frame a dusting and hope his time would come quickly. I watched spellbound. Those strong firm jaws, and that high forehead slowly seemed to yield to a phantom sculptor. "Mr. President, we all knew you to be a strong statesman." Now you must go with the flow, so to speak. And go he did.

I took a break for my tea and pie. The fire was warm, the windows reflected its hearty flicker. Within all was well.

Crash!

I spun about, slopped tea into the fire, and dropped pieces of pie onto Noel's carpet into the bargain. The noise was much more than a single falling comrade. It was a whole length of window frame splintered, and fallen into the room. Affixed to it, as testimony to the hand that dealt such ferocity, was a large shattered tree limb.

There was no time to waste. I grabbed what wraps I had at hand and ran outside for a tarp or canvas from the nearby outbuilding. Wind fought me all the way and I was awash from bow to stern, as I raced the wilderness which attempted to articulate my body parts into distant places yet unknown, to explorers and missionaries.

Inside again, I stuffed canvas into the remains of a once beautiful leaded glass window. The limb rested on the floor. How ironic. Here

I am, searching in vain for missing fallen comrades inside, while from outside enters the limb of an unknown donor flying through a window. It had rested amidst a gathering of rainwater, smashed glass and the very late Sir. Winston Churchill. I suspect he found the similarity to the London Blitz too much, and being a bit on the heavy side, rather than being blown away, he dropped to earth, corpse-like.

The picture frame was uneventful in its survival; intact and empty as it was. Of course, I felt much the same, here I was, still lasting out the storm and feeling totally remote.

I asked the gasping octogenarian I had become, "Why me, and why this way?"

The walls took the 5th and remained silent as mice. Well why not, most of the mice in this castle having died, along with the cat and the occupants, many of them anyway, it did appear. I was scared but darn angry too. I had felt akin to Winston, having served under his *Home Guard* during the blitz. Now he was gone and not even a photo left.

I have gone way off the deep end now. For starts, these photos were not of the actual people; I know that for a fact. I also know that in so far as time is concerned, at the moment I entered this dwelling place, Mr. Churchill was in fact healthy and living a somewhat secluded life in Falmouth. When I get out of this I shall call upon him and relay all of this strange story. Perhaps we will laugh over a cup of tea. Perhaps not, also.

I still have to account for the fact that when I was outside searching for a window covering, I realized that my rented Humber had disappeared. Now that would not just *drop off the wall*, nor would wind take the old machine off down the road. For some reason, I was abandoned to reside here for the duration; how long that might be was anybody's guess. I wanted to leave prior to joining old friends who had recently departed the bleak portrait walls.

Curiosity, more than the wrenching cold, drove me back inside after my efforts to staunch the flow of rainwater from invading through the smashed opening in the wall, once site of a beautiful leaded glass. I was drawn back to my family with the realization that time was not in their favor. The benediction had better be ready. They would fair no better than a candle in a hurricane.

The next to go would most certainly be Edward de Vere, aka William Shakespeare. The 52 years did not hang well on this man. He had written 36 plays, 154 sonnets, and vastly more. His pen was soon to fall silent.

Again, I was drawn to a mad rush of sounds from without; I watched wild wind take small debris and send it toward sky's blackened zenith. I watched the sky full of clouds incensing an enraged rush toward a maddened clash with the heavens. I listened as thundering messages from above arrived complete with flashing light to read them by. I wondered about time, space, life as it was now and later life too. Questions about heaven seemed appropriate.

Crash!

The north wall received a touch of earth-bound fire. The flames within the fireplace vanished, exploded, relit and roared into an inferno enough to lighten my black quarters into a daylight not seen now for some days.

I glanced briefly at William. In that instant there was time to blink, straighten one's back, take a bite of air and light out on a short speech. He selected naught a word, looked skyward and slumped into the darkened recesses of time.

The quality of mercy is not strained... However I hoped some had in fact, *...fallen like gentle rains from heaven...* upon him. His picture fairly flew off the wall, slapped the fireside stones with a resounding explosion, and danced briefly, *Clitus: Fly, my lord, fly!* I hoped the wings of departure took William Edward de Vere Shakespeare aloft to "... share the glories of (these) happy days." Alas poor William, I knew him not, but it was the heaviest loss to take so far and the room was in mourning for hours. At Hedingham Castle, the flag was dropped to half-mast. My friends, who remained, and I had a solemn tea that afternoon. These deaths were very hard on all of us. I hoped that this one had been the last. I held out in vain.

At 4:30, as the day began to grow still bleaker, conditions within worsened. I realized that it was not going well in the northeast corner. The candle in the hall burnt black, the curtains refused to stay open, a door into gloomy storage beneath the stair slammed open and closed continually. Cold in that area, just east of the fireplace, was severe.

Heavy frost remained as a drape on the walls and slid downward to the floors; remained there even during the daytime. Worse, it was spreading into the otherwise still living reaches of the fireside room.

I could say Henry VIII was my least favorite "family member" to grace the walls. That would be unfair and might in fact cast suspicion as to whether I in fact initiated the following incident. I did not.

Truth to tell, I was back to the fire and sipping a cuppa, when I realized that Henry was rocking in his frame on the wall. With reluctance, I approached the area for a closer look. His head hung at a rakish angle, while flowing downward from the frame was a soft patina of red. The frame rocked slowly on its wire hanger, made one maddened flip and dashed to the fire for the "roasting of the king." I made a dizzy lunge for the frame, flung it onto the fireside rug and dashed off the flames with my handkerchief. The damage was done. The only thing to remain was Henry's head balanced conspicuously on the brink of the frame. In an instant that too began vanishing along with his hulk, his name and his fame.

*Nothing remained beyond, save the lone and level sand*s... (Percy Shelly on kings and kingdoms that proposed to be invincible.)

I was left holding all that remained of the once proud and ambitious king who banished heads of state, heads of church and heads of wives. His last act, perhaps a symbolic leap into the fires of hell, was bested only by his remaining head, which I exhibited on the mantle for the brief time it took for it also to vanish. Sorry Henry, no 30 days stay on Executioner's Gate for you. In time, I would rehang his very obviously empty frame on the wall and gasp at the effect upon the surroundings.

The log-fire flamed with renewal, walls and floorboards sheathed in ice melted, doors functioned normally and nearby on their wood stands, candles burned livelier once again.

The afternoon moved into evening and bled a weakened flicker of darkened sun touching frosted panes. Daylight became just a joke adrift someplace above. Gradually however, heat from the fireplace soaked up my rain-damp clothing and I felt some warmth return.

The glass of the first president's photograph yet lingered in a soft cloak of frost. George was always warm in life. Today, he appeared a cold statesman and a bleak hope for the First Continental Congress.

Perhaps I should remember, this is not *our* George Washington; just a chilled and ponderous look-alike. I brushed aside the heaviness of the moment and went right to the man himself. The *Father of Our Country* was balding nicely, held only a thin line against a sterner face and gazed slightly to our right, the *Republican Right* one can but hope. He held aloft no torch for separation of powers, was not a state's rights man and indeed blamed antifederalists for any failure present or future by those who spoke out for such.

The scullery beckoned. I parted with Mr. Washington, feeling a stronger man by our time spent together. I was ready to face any separation of power betwixt myself from this dungeon of horrors and death. George held high the banner of independence and freedom. I was such a fellow; one for all and all for one, *Up the Nation* and all that.

I almost shouted, but checked myself in puzzlement. Who was I to be brave at so bleak and dark a moment? I was not a revolutionist and could never hold a candle to the nation, much less myself. The image had faded, was slipping, had lost most of its warmth. George tugged at my sleeve, at my conscience, at my counterpoise. Never one to sit upon the fence, he willed me to jump right in and stir up the embers and enliven the insurrection against the hand that wrought such negation against man's freedom from tyranny. I was weak and faltered.

I made a chilled observation. One glance at the nation's first and I realized time was short. What the winter at Valley Forge did not do for Mr. President, a cold afternoon in *The Shutters* had succeeded in accomplishing in only a few chilled and impersonal hours. He was pinched, gaunt, looking bent and dehydrated. I would caution the voters: "Mr. Washington might not make his second term of office."

I dreaded the time spent separated from my nation's first leader, but selected to have my tea at fireside. I was again feeling the cold. The strain of the hours past aged me, so too the onward caravan to some end unknown to all but Noel; and he was missing from the stage.

Scones discovered in a breadbox were heated and buttered and served (by myself, thank you) to elevate my wilting emotions.

Meanwhile, my mental state must have received a boost as suddenly I realized that certainly there must be a phone, a radio or a wireless-set about the place. Noel could not have lived here, remote as it was, without some form of contact with the "outside world." The ancient three tube radio, when I found it in a tired and chilled corner of his snug, was cold to the touch, silent to the ear and dead as the bodies on the wall.

I screamed, just to clear the air, just to move aside the closeness of the impending horror I expelled forth my pent-up fear of such desolation; just to confirm that I was alive and had not slipped into my own "frame," I screamed.

A loud thump from a dark wall fireside in the living room drew my attention to the framed photograph of our original political leader. He indeed was finished.

Thomas Jefferson wrote of George Washington: *He never acted until every circumstance was weighed.* I guess until that moment he too hoped against hope for some alternate solution to the blight which ripped from our surroundings so many fine gentlemen (as well as a few slightly less adequate.) His was a quiet finish. Upon discovering that he was very ill, he held off having Martha call for medical assistance. He slipped away on a cold and bleak day in the late afternoon.

I went to check the date upon a calendar posted in the scullery; yep, it was Monday, December 12th.

Against the far-side newel post hung the yet surviving Napoleon Bonaparte. He maintained an unusual silence. Perhaps, for once, he had no opposing opinion. Perhaps he bowed to the passing of our late national leader. Perhaps he realized the implications of that latest demise; his photo was next in line!

The photo of Napoleon Bonaparte, the short egomaniac from Corsica, Italy, hung high on the wall, as well it might. Napoleon, as was his birth name, was short in stature, although very high in his opinion of himself. To properly view his photo one must stand on toes and look up, way up. The Iconoclastic Revolution had not touched Napoleon. The people will remain dominated and downtrodden. The mighty will bask aloof in pulpits of elevated grander, if only self-elevated. Napoleon looked worried. Perhaps he still held out hope for the rains to cease and the defeat of Wellington at Waterloo to go as planned. (Well, that's another game cancelled due to rain.)

Outside of my own Waterloo, rains continue also, as does the sleet and wind. It had become a wetness without and within. I felt moisture inside closed cupboards, within my clothing and running off the window dressings. Perhaps Napoleon, here ensconced, holds out for brighter days. In his altered state, he appears somewhat slumped. His three cornered hat is askew. His Epicurean paunch seems a bit depleted. No saber is scabbarded at his side, and his epaulets are tarnished. The short dictator's appearance is a little too general for too little a general.

I launch myself to the fireside to pile more wood onto the waning pyre. There is a loud splash and a resounding thud from behind me. I need not hasten to turn about. A dashed plan, prepared in haste, ill health and plans undertaken with poor training has left my latest companion awash on the flooring of *The Shutters*. General Bonaparte had met his Waterloo and taken part of it with him to the lowest point of his falsely elevated career. Down off the pedestal came Napoleon and dashed onto floorboards that have hosted some of the greatest and the least of us. His frame is bent, damp and empty. His too is an uncertain rest, but join the proletariat he must.

Night is upon me in all of her gloom and renewed frenzy of storm. Punctual in her regime she will throw in a handful of horrors to match any footpath through death's door. I have steeled myself for this time. There is one photograph left; well, there is one photo plus a blank frame.

That lends me no alacrity to a peaceful passing. Rather, it gives rise to more trepidation on my part. I, after all, need give rise to hope in this battleship of terrors and death. Welled up from within, the hope seems to perish as a flame doffs its glow to a hurricane...quenched. I digress, more from distraught than lacking.

To the scullery once more for a supper. The faces on the walls were more comfort. This solitary insanity is a portion to be shared. Battled alone, any storm need give homage to faith, hope and forbearance although I have some time yet it would appear. Tomorrow I will light out, in whatever weather for help, company and comfort. It cannot be so far a walk to the gate-keepers house, perhaps two miles. If the storm abates I intend to light out at daybreak.

Now, for a light meal. The scullery, when I ventured inside, was fairly awash with leaks. It would appear that a sea wall had capsized somewhere off to the east and let in the tides. The floor ran with water in pools and rivulets. Small breakers seemed to dance at me from the far doorway. I tried to pull fast the ports and latch them as best I could. It seemed to only bring forth a renewed onslaught of inundation.

I decided on supper at the fireside and cold cut sandwiches again. There was a hanger on the hearth for a jug and hot water was not far off. I built up the blaze for comfort, for warmth, for camaraderie, for something to do with my worried hands.

The time for action was spent and now my spirits, trapped within, gave vent to demands unfulfilled. I should be on the road and making fast for a place of light and hope. I could not. Within was courage but without courage was without my whole self. My entire frame creaked of pent-up dreams, ambitions and hopes. The period of accomplishments perhaps had passed, not unlike the passing of my companions; and with their passing, I was launched into the end of my journey. I saw myself in the frames too, dashed on the floorboards, dead in the water, dead in fact. Was this then the aim of this entire venture, interned in darkness and solitary until the surrounding mood of somber horrors and death drove me over the edge to my own…finish, obliteration, death? And at my own hands perhaps?

Back into the room of the burning logs and dying cellmates, I glanced at the remaining face framed on those stained-oak plank walls, and with some astonishment realized it beckoned me to draw near, nearer. The survivor waved about on its wire, not unlike an acrobat on a suspension cable, walking above the entranced crowds. I looked at the face of a vastly-aged Noel. It was a ramshackle wreckage-investiture, heaped upon the former person I had known. Time had not been good to him. Ha! Time had in fact played a dirty trick on him, and lumped all of its left-over ages upon his façade. The dumping grounds of wrinkles, wrath, and the chaff of ages all begot that ruination of repulse personified. The master who controlled this time machine of aghast human distortion saved till the last what was in fact the first really brutal and inhuman treatment of the portraits.

I returned in sickness to my fireside seat and wept. This way was to ruination for sure. I must take control. The wave came in from the scullery and brought new bother and fear. I ached for some hope, for my lost cellmates, for company; all of which in dashed reprise lay elsewhere for me on that darkened day. I suffered as only one in hell can finally do so. The current ran faster. I longed to breathe deeply of that cold salt water and find fresh release and finality from the peace thereby brought. I did not.

Crash!

Slam!

"Oooooohhhhhhhhhhhhhhhhhhhh!"

I fairly shrank inside with fear of what waited, and watched. I was not alone now. There were eight missing and one almost dead in my dungeon. Also, there was the element of surprise in the wings of this drama unfolding. I dreaded that specter most of all. What is, can be dealt with. *"Heard sounds are sweet, those unheard are sweeter."* Thank you Mr. Shakespeare, however, too little too late and I wish that unheard would remain just that. Once delivered, that unknown has a pall of the unearthly, undesirable and therefore that unheard sound is a terror for the heart.

The last photo dropped.

The last friend, if friend he be, was no more.

I wasted no time in planning for his burial. The frame must be cleaned and dressed. Perhaps something light for so dark a moment when he passed. I was becoming rather demented now. Fully aware of such made me sane in the textbooks. However, in fact, I was a completely deranged, frenzied lunatic. Any hopes of exploit was over with. Anything left was reaction. I dropped into my old leather chair. I vanished.

A door slammed.

I stirred slightly. Footfalls on the old oak floors silenced the gloom of hush which had gowned my body, my circumstances and the ambient storm of my life.

Noel had returned.

Upon his entry he would discover my gaunt remainder slumped in a fireside chair, ancient and dazed. A very low point indeed, having aged vastly more than just days during those forty-eight hours. My person, simply reduced in strength and stature, rested deeper, deeper into fabric folds of some late beast who gave all for my deep accommodation at fireside.

Noel walked in, looking far too young and fresh for his years. He arrived as if it had been simply a moment's pause in a lengthy conversation, rather than years since last we met.

No introduction, he jumped right in with both feet; "So, did you enjoy your stay? And what about my photo collection, did it amuse you?"

As he spoke, he eagerly strode about the room, gazing into each photo frame. I was prepared for the worst. I realized that it was I who attended the loss of each entry in his collection of photographs. It was I who was responsible for the death of the nine, and perhaps the loss of one other too. I was none too eager to engage in this conversation and felt remote from this young version of a former elderly cousin.

"Err, that is, how are you Noel? I have not seen you for a few years and time has been good to you."

He was not going to sip even a morsel of it, he did not accept my apologetic tone. I was wallowing in self-pity and self-incrimination before a stone icon. He had no use for it at all.

"Oh, come on now Francis, do you really think Noel is only 34 years old today? Give it up. You are far smarter and although currently looking a bit bashed, far quicker too." He was involved in a conversation with someone who was no longer present.

I arose, a doddering gentleman, ostensibly well into my 90's for sure. I grasped the table edge for support and began to advance to the scullery door.

"Those photos..." I began. "They all disappeared, all rather suddenly, don't you see?"

I was panting, almost lost in blustering emotion. The sweeping panoramic view of the room disclosed the full nine photos, all framed, glassed and exactly as previously hung. In my diminished vision I even fantasized a 10th frame, housing a final face. I gasped, tottered and all but collapsed into a slumped posture of release. Back into the worn leather chair I sank; my home throughout these past painful, no, mournful hours. Somehow my vision began to fade, my breath emitted a mere cobweb of a gasp.

"Well," Noel began; only of course he was not, never had been Noel. "Perhaps you should enlighten me as to why you came for that visit, visit to your favorite cousin Noel, visit which you had put off for so many years. And can you even explain why you never left after that?"

In a futile attempt to survive this notion of a diminished mental capacity, I discovered myself drifting into a dim recess, into a pocket of time saved just for those in their final stages. I glimpsed a distant trace of time and energy, then, even that deteriorated into a dot and then - into nothing.

Noel, the only name I can ever know him by, lifted the 10th framed photo from the wall. "Here, look at this photo, a good likeness of someone you knew in life."

He waved it about like a bloody butcher paper. "It shall hang with the collection of the others who visited me and never left."

His tone, his entire attitude transitioned at that point from slightly removed to vicious and vindictive. "The others who hang on the walls, rest in the cellars, cellars of my house, not Noels' house, not his inheritance, mine! You always had everything, Francis. Noel was the fair-haired cousin, Francis the worthy son. I was left to starve in that crumbling counting house in Farnsworth. You remember now? Does it all come back? Now who's laughing? Huh? Huh?"

I receeded farther. I was a drooping worm on the hook and the shark was by my side ready to bolt down. I slipped farther back. Dirk, Dirk Van Dunn, the no-account son of my father's first wife. He who stood before the magistrate and swore revenge when we processed him for pilfering thousands from the bookkeeping firm we owned in years past. Dirk, returned from exile in Australia and living in the home of Noel. And what of Noel?"

"Oh, sit there and listen a bit." He piped. "You must have this all mapped out. You, who always knew the answers and glad-handed himself into the seat of honor at father's firm. Ha! Where has it all gotten you now? Huh? Well, look closely at those photos."

He waved an arrogant arm about at *The Ten* framed on the walls and chuckled an evil tone.

"I've collected them over the years. Know them all you think, sure? Well, look again. There," he pointed to where Mr. President George Washington had hung, "there is Uncle Fritz. And there," his arm continued its' gesturing attitude, "there are cousins Justin and Herb.

Still further, that frog-faced old bat, that one, who looks like Winnie, well he was your barrister, the one who pointed the finger at me at the magistrate's dock. He sleeps in the cellars with the rest now. Bugger the lot! And look, that picture there," his hand, claw-like, gestured toward that tenth frame. "I'll just bet you think it's an inadequate portrait of Noel. Well, no luck, and no photo of him either. Oh, he's gone for certain, just not immortalized on these walls but forever gone."

He made a maddened flick of the wrist toward a far-side door in the darkened corner of the room. "He was the last to go but one; he's resting down in the crypt with the others. Now, one more guest to file down the stairs and join the family tree, if tree it be, then climb upon your limb dear Francis 'cause it's your turn now."

His voice elevated toward a hideous scream. "See that final photo, well look carefully; see him, huh, huh, see him?" He snatched the astonishingly poignant photo from its hook on the wall and brandished it before my failing vision, leered at me with a forbidding smirk. "So, who is that specter?"

I gazed in blanched trepidation. My muddled mind and faltering step took me toward the 10th frame. That final photo, always elusive, always empty, always the pivotal point in the gallery of revere and dread. The famous photo, no doubt a statesman, perhaps a field marshal.

I looked closely. Time was sluggish now. I pulled myself up on my toes and gazed eye-to-eye with...myself! It was my own face looking back, death-like now, far gone into frailty and gaunt did I return the gaze.

The splendor of years past was definitely past, vanished, extinct. I was the old gomer we always look away from on the street, in the bread queue, on the trolley. I was the last item left in the family line.

Now the way was clear. Now the entire estate would revert to the sole survivor. Not to Noel, no, he was resting in dirt in the darkened cellars. No, the entire Macbeth Fabrications Ltd. fortune now reverted to...Dirk Van Dunn.

I slumped deeper now, was far gone and peaceful in my dot in time and space. Dirk sauntered about the room, replaced the photo in the 10th frame again on its nail, switched off the lights, ushered in the final darkness.

A few coals fell on the grate, a log dropped into a recess in the fireplace, fell into ashes, into dust to soon join me in timeless dirt and dust below cellar floors. It was silent now save for a mournful clock in a dismal hallway, distantly ticking off some score of finality, seconds, seconds, seconds. Time had her turn at last, as in her twisted manner, she, crept upon us each. My peace was at hand, my turn to visit the darkness eternal was momentary. My vulnerability was done.

Dirk drew tight the curtains and paused for a farewell. "Francis, bugger you and all like you. Take this curse for all your type."

His jeer echoed across the darkened gloom of the great room, "While I escort you down to join a sea of dead bodies, take this thought to your grave. I, in the end, I was stronger, the survivor, and the winner, while you and your softness just lost it all. Ha!"

He grasped the nearby door knob with an offensive hand, turned with parting mockery, casting his last my way and wretched open the door to depart. "Damn you Francis, get ready for... ...aaahhhhhhhh..."

Dirk should have taken time to get in touch with his house. He missed the front door, missed an innocent closet door too, and in his arrogance and haste wretched open the cellar door. In his flight, he cleared the stone steps, all 24 of them, and buried himself into the cobbles and dirt eighteen feet below. It required only locating the shovel and finishing his grave. No long box, no floral wreath, no line of moist-eyed mourners. Dirk went out, not with a triumphant cheer but with a dying curse.

I sat silently then. There was no rush. The family had gathered for my burial and got instead the no-good stepson. It remained only to explain the other nine bodies to the authorities. I suspect I will think upon that one for a spell.

Outside the rain had stopped.

BAND PRACTICE MAYHEM

At the root of our plan, well more like a scheme, was to overcome the boredom of fifth grade band practice, cook up a plot to win the battle against the system, and come out laughing hysterically in the end.

We gathered together each day in our really rough bandhall, which was filled with cool places to hide as well as a mess of half-broken music stands, half-missing band books, broken pencils, and unaccounted for practice logs usually with no name on them. You'd also find a jumble of chairs where the musicians, and those who played saxophone (ha ha), gathered to hear Master Lander bust out with a loud chorus of, "Turn to page 42 and we will open with the b-flat scale. Let's try to do it all together; no popcorn starts and no chaotic endings." The director had not had his morning coffee, hence he was not in his best disposition.

Things progressed as usual, with clarinet players frantically looking for lost reeds, saxophones searching for that key on the backside to make an octave change, while someplace in the back of the band-hall, a maniac with long blond hair was bashing the kit into an admix of broken bicycle wheels, old leftover McDonalds *unhappy* meals and damaged Volkswagen parts suspended in 7/8 time. As always, those of us in the exclusive low brass section were sitting in typically illegal posture. We were hiding from our music while still blasting deep bass notes, and looking around in surprise when the director said to, "Remove temptation from your mouth."

The euphonium player was endeavoring to hack to death a music stand, which refused to function as anything but bent metal, while dumping his spit valves on the shoes of nearby musicians unfortunate enough to be seated within spitting distance; all of which made a joy of playing anything with a spit valve. Discarded liquid flew, music pages flipped in 4/4 time and eventually we were anointed with a piece which somehow represented at least some of what the composer had in mind low those many years past.

Meanwhile, several musicians had collapsed into narcolepsy, albeit no different from their usual state of existence, and the entire band and the percussionist were dismissed to stand down, while those with mouthpieces and sticky valves were allowed to baptize them with oils and alcoholic sanitizer.

In a gulp one trumpet player, not to be named, consumed his entire bottle of sanitizer and was later seen leaning against the drinking fountain and mumbling something about an "old coat." Throughout the brass section spit valves were emptied in a frenzy of *baptize the musicians in front of you*, then look at the person to your left in an accusatory manner. It always worked.

The director was back on his stand with an eye out for posture and eyes anyplace but on the baton in his hands. In weaker moments he would pass temporary directorship of the band to various members, a decision he would regret for years to come.

In the corner of the bandhall and perched precariously atop an ancient, *Meyers Brothers* of New York three-legged baby grand piano of some questionable origin, stood the traditional music department Christmas tree (purchased online, no doubt) and bedizened with gaudy decorations left over from a stage production of the *Maldonado* Opera of 1873, and surrounded by suspiciously artificial gifts.

Rumor had it that the piano once excited crowds of Can-Can dancers in the '30's, in a brothel on Sanchez Street, off Market in San Francisco.

The three student *directors* took over and attacked the leadership of the mob with all the finesse of a sinking aircraft carrier in a storm at sea; that is to say they had no hope from the beginning.

"Turn in your books to page 63 and play the first two lines of the Etude, *Anasthasia*, from the opera *Arianna in Paris,* and remember to count to yourselves as we direct it up here. That means you will need to use what Mr. Smith?"

Mr. Smith, resting in a most unmusical posture, was engaged in the all-time favorite game of *hide the music case* of the person in front of you. He was rooting around under chairs, cautiously sliding someone's empty clarinet case toward a new home yards away beneath the piano. The entire back row of brass and woodwinds endured hysteria and failed to hide it. The joke went, *Don't look at the trombones, it will only encourage them.*

As the leaders announced *instruments up* and the baton dropped for the opening note, which on the score was indicated as *piano* but came across as a mixture of *cacophony and triple fortissimo*, a small riot erupted between a trumpet and a clarinet, rapidly escalated into mayhem as the entire *woodwind* section, moved like a forest fire into *brass*, and ended up with the stands and music from the entire back row making a move for the door, while dragging with them empty cases, a timpani, the percussion box, one drummer dressed in a perplexed state of astonishment, numerous coats, music folders, and a few unsuspecting music students who were actually engaged in following the score and the directors. The remaining students were swept south and east, engulfed the piano, the remains of the Christmas tree including ancient decorations and faux gifts in bedraggled dressing, the three directors, complete with faux laughter, their stand and an awash array of what would, under normal circumstances, pass for timesheets and instruction notes, and lastly Master Lander himself, finally holding a mug of steaming tea and a mostly distraught look on his face. Giving up all controls he had time to shout: "...and on the count of three and not a second sooner, get out of here and have a **Merry Christmas!**"

GETTING PLASTERED IN THE HALLS

S he continued to scream, the childlike voice resonating off the newly- plastered walls and dropping onto dead-tired time-disgraced carpeting.

"Someone stole my lighter, my lighter. Does anyone care, does anyone give a bloody rip about my lighter?"

She wavered about the hall a bit and continued, now in a falsetto whine, "My lighter is gone, and so is my coin! I'm broke and I can't smoke and since obviously no one loves me; there isn't much else to do so I'm leaving!"

I continued to scrape off old paint and prepare the aging walls for a coat of new plaster and color. Guests at the facility all wanted pink, green, yellow, or white. The boss said, "Same color as before, which to my eye read as a sort of washed-out light beige. (It doesn't help that I'm quite color blind too.)

The front door shoved open, admitting a late November wind to assault the halls and escort in blowing snow as well. It closed with an intensified slam, reverberated throughout the entire front room, where snoozing in threadbare recliners the gathered guests were not stimulated; rather they remained half asleep, ears only faintly tuned-in to daily radio broadcasts of *Alles mein guten Tag.*

It wasn't such a great loss. Peggy Wilford left the facility daily, and returned as often (more is the pity some might say.)The lodge where

Peggy "lived" was a small private care facility for those with less than a full bank account and for some a slightly less-than-full-deck too. Peggy was a fairly typical guest, and while a prime target for endless imagined assaults, was in fact just another member of the old-cloth-and-socks that wandered the halls of the *Goldene Lebensjahre* care facility, an elderly haven for war survivors and street tenants. It was situated in a long-closed winery huddled on fourteen acres of apple trees, also desolate, or bombed, or burned or whatever was their demise during the war. Maintenance was deferred for "another time." Meanwhile, the entire layout progressively glided downhill toward the rusting rails of the *Deutsche Eisenbahnwerkstatten,* a seldom used freight spur, situated four kilometers outside the small town of Singen, in southern Germany.

At the *Goldene Lebensjahre,* I worked as a part-time plasterer/painter, a job which posed a daily challenge to determine exactly who needed to be interned, the guests, the staff, or me.

My fulltime job as mid-watch air-ops despatcher for NavAirArm at nearby Aeyeredang Air Force Base left my days free for hiking, mountain climbing, and painting.

Goldene Lebensjahre was owned and managed by my lifelong friend Gerk Eisenberg. When he called with a suggestion of part-time income in exchange for my painting skills …I couldn't say no. Oh more the fool I for extra money.

"Waah waah waaaaaaa. Secrets, secrets, I've got secrets!" Edson was at it again, wandering the halls and vomiting her boisterous tirades.

During the qualifying interview, the staff realized that she alone of the three women recently transferred from a facility in England, stood little chance for any form of rehabilitation. Edson's mind wandered, along with her body, strapped in a bath chair; meanwhile, her busy feet propelled her about the halls spreading joy to all she encountered.

I moved aside, and dragged my tarp and buckets with me. No need make a further mess which I might be in command of cleaning up.

"Waah waah waaaaaaah!"

Of the other two patients she had arrived with, one was well on her way to being discharged and a placement in the job field. Her sister however, was almost totally blind, had one leg, and was burned over about forty percent of her body. She had a kind disposition but was unable to speak due, scant records indicated, to inhalation of superheated smoke, subsequent to some form of aircraft accident.

It was five years since the war had ended, leaving a good portion of Germany, as well as Edson and thousands like her, in a state of mental collapse, hence there was typically a full house at the care facility.

I was making my way further down the main entry hall, filling small cracks and caulking corners, when I encountered *Sticks*. *Sticks* Hudson was a relatively incoherent six-foot three-inches tall, weighed about 125 pounds, and endlessly roamed the halls of the facility searching for a corner.

He demanded two walls, preferably at right angles to give him a *safe corner* in which to linger, but only briefly. His eyes were always on the search for the next safe square on the checkerboard of life. This represented his everyday progress from front door, to front living room, to front dining room, to restroom, to day room, and his bedroom and then, in a full reverse pattern, back toward the big glass front door. Hudson seldom remained immobile for long as he progressed along the main street of his focused destination.

In his mind there were certain forces at work in his pathway, and were he to linger too long at any corner, *they* would get him and he would be dragged out into the center of the hallway without a corner in sight, and according to him, "I'd be all sucked dry!" His enemies lived under his bed, along with his *Treasures*, and were called *Beaches* and had a fixation on his legs. (Those spindles of hairless necrotic skin supporting his frail 125-pound skeleton.) At any time during the day Hudson might be found hugging a corner and speculating on the next move, while keeping a weathered eye out for *them blasted beaches.*

I apologize for painting (said the painter) so grim a nightmare of tattered and wasted humanity, but in fact that is the closest form of description available for the lost and outcast citizens residing at the *Goldene Lebensjahre.* There were a few slightly less eccentric types in attendance. They were the workers.

"Guests," as the residents at the facility were called, were allowed to meet with a member of the staff at the office during the day to make or receive phone calls, order prescriptions (when approved by their physician), check on the status of a visitor, a package, or some mail.

While this was normal guest conduct, it typically took on a restless and often confrontational attitude, usually depending on the outcome of the guest's quarry.

"I want my prescription refilled." A typical demand from Karley Crocodile, so named by the other guests, (and if the truth were known by members of the staff too,) for her jaws of steel; Karley bites!

"That doc didn't leave me my meds. I asked him time after time and still he refuses to leave me any meds for my nerves."

She pounded on the wall, an as yet unpainted section of the hallway located just outside the secretary's office, and waited, as if expecting her doctor to magically appear through the wall bearing a vile of her favorite *nerve medicine* on demand.

"I pay my bills, so I demand my rights. Where is that doctor? Where are my meds?" Screams now. "He hates me, yep that's it. Blasted doctor hates me and so…he withholds my meds." (Darling, if anyone is punished by your not taking medication, real or fancied, it would be the gathered multitudes at the *Goldene Lebensjahre.)*

Gerk and two angelic doyennes, sisters Winnie and Wilma Bergdorf, plus a staff of about twenty, ran the facility day and night. Well, it would suffice to say they *directed* activities. There were more than a few "guests" who "ran things" if truth be known.

Three of these aides, Hilda, Margaret, and Hazel were in charge of social events and scheduled such community gatherings as: exercise class on Mondays at three pm, manicures on Tuesday, Bingo on Wednesday afternoon (although Bingo could pop up at any moment the Bingo Club decided to hold a competition,) and music on Thursday afternoons.

And then there was the cooking class, mostly the eating of raw dough and the few surviving cookies which actually made it into the ovens, but a cooking class none-the-less, held each Friday afternoon to get everyone well stocked with sugar. Shock time for the PM shift on Friday as the mob descended on the dining hall for dinner following a full two hours of mixing, tasting, and eating the well- sugared extravagances from the "gastronomic arts conservatory" of the *Goldene Lebensjahre.*

"She ate my cookies, blast her eyes, she ate my cookies and I'm going to rip out her heart in exchange!" Myrtle was off her meds and stuffed to the eyeballs with rocket power (sugar) and feeling shorted by at least one, two inch flat white flower and sugar cookie; she was ready to do war.

"Hey, you, Hank, you take care of this right now or I swear I will jump on her, and you know from past experience I'm capable of causing unspeakable bodily damage!"

Yep, Myrtle had gone a few rounds with *Teddy Roosevelt* and he had come up second with a very sore finger and a bloody nose. That battle had been over a "stolen" coffee cup which Teddy carried around since joining the home, talked to endlessly and sipped from it whatever was at hand: coffee, tea, water, juices, he drank 'em all.

Teddy Roosevelt was the name he arrived with, and no other name being available, he was accepted as Teddy. He never recognized his own name, but within days of arrival had memorized the names of many staff members as well as most other guests too. Teddy, ragged, rugged, unkempt, and rough in tongue and nature, thought that his dirty and well-chewed paper cup was his wife, and while he had acquired it from a dumpster outside a Mövenpeck restaurant, he persisted in the belief that the cup was his long lost wife. Meanwhile, mainly when off her meds, Myrtle chased him around in a vein effort to recover the cup which she was certain was part of the Wedgewood *Kingsbridge* pattern of dishes which she had rescued from the ocean liner *Il de France* prior to World War II.

The hallways rang with her unceasing cries and curses, doors opened and slammed in staccato rhythm as Teddy came and went in failed attempts to escape, and the two gave a fairly accurate replay of an early 1900's American black and white slap-stick comedy starring *Laurel and Hardy*.

While many of the guests ambulated about with wheelchairs, walkers or canes, many were just slow movers and a few were not even remotely handicapped.

Working in the halls always involved moving paint, tarps, plaster, tools, and foremost as this was "their" home, I was alert to not get in anyone's way.

On his good days, Teddy, enjoyed life in an endless wandering indoors and out while ceaselessly prattling. I got a lot done on those days; less time spent rescuing paint and plaster from the stampeding feet of Teddy and Myrtle through my nervous halls of plastering struggle. When weather allowed, not during snowstorms, I was also working on the exterior of the facility which gave me a fair degree of audience to Teddy's outdoor exhibitions as well. Some days he was in charge of loading freight at a railroad terminal with shouts and curses as imagined workers failed to get things right.

"Take it over there, no not that car stupid, over there, the freight car with J0001742 stamped on the side." He had a system of numbers known only to himself, but if you tracked him over the course of a day there was a pattern to them. "Get on with it, move it; we have aircraft engines to load too!"

The typical day moved toward midday and lunch-time rolled around with all the pulling of teeth involved in getting the overweight as well as the anorexic to come to mealtime. It wasn't the food, although on occasion it might have been a cause for a lesser person to remain room-bound with the door locked and feigning extreme intestinal malaise. The guests at the "home" just didn't tend to organize well, get together, form groups, or stand in lines; on different days it might be for food, for showers, for meds.

So, Hazel or Hank moved from room to room, from group to group and announced, "Lunch time dear, come to lunch now," and in a kindness only those two could pull off with any of the guests: Sticks, Karley, or Teddy, having received a kind and gentle urging, prayerfully arrived for the meal in a passive temper.

"What, not this again. No I can't stand it, and what's more, upon my rights as a paying resident here, I hereby refuse to eat it!" Wow, only slightly short of any degree of jocularity; Teddy was not having a good day, and was not of a "passive temper" by far. His hand shot out and the grilled cheese sandwich flew across the room and landed on the plate of Freda Ryan Lampshade, who was overweight by a couple of stones and could easily do without one sandwich, never mind two.

"Oh Ducks, thanks ever so; why, this is just what I need, hungry girl as I seem to be today."

Today? Well yes today, and yesterday, and tomorrow and next summer on any day with a "Y" in it too. Freda was unable to hold back when food was involved and as such dressed in circus tents, or so rumor went. Actually, they were massive table cloths donated by a catering service which folded its doors in a building not far away, and "bestowed" massive amounts of goods upon the facility, including huge round green tablecloths. A pair of scissors, a large hole in the center for the head and behold, Freda, in a new garb.

Oh yes, her last name. Well, her last name was Hovendyke, but you see, Freda had a fetish. She loved lampshades and always wore one of her garish collection of a couple dozen of them as a fashionable pinnacle, day in and day out. She had one for Easter, Christmas, Guy Fawkes Day, Winter Solstice and more. If she appeared sans fashionable headdress, she was either in the shower or asleep.

Freda wore a massive piece of World War I military headgear for shower time, but she was one of the lady guests who was able to shower unassisted,

Therefore, no one but a member of the staff, who accidently opened the shower door during the "sacred scrub down," was privy to Freda's version of the *Water Symphony Suit,* a nocturnal event designed to send G.F. Handel scurrying back to his pianoforte for decomposition.

Mealtime progressed; Teddy made due with a bowl of tomato soup and crackers, and Freda was cajoled into sharing her second Käsesandwich with Liza of the skin and bones family of non-eaters. There were three of them in residence at the *Goldene Lebensjahre* and mealtime for them was like a fasting for us normal eaters, an event to avoid at any cost.

Many of the guests entered a form of dreamland after meals, particularly the noon-time meal. (A time when I had the halls to myself and made fair progress in plaster, paint and trim work.) The guests frequently retired to their rooms for a nap, or went out to the patios for a smoke and light conversation,

A few moved down the halls to the radio lounges for what passed for entertainment on daytime radio, and a few sat quietly in the halls and gazed. The time-consuming art of gazing for the guests might be called reading, daydreaming, creative thinking, or mulling over an idea or project.

Guests at the *Goldene Lebensjahre* did very little creative thinking and discussions were on the level of me, mine, you, yours, she said, he said, and they said or did. It just remained on the very basic personal pronoun level of thinking.

Very often, when talking with some of the guests they became very animated and excited because, for them, personal interaction was a challenge and posed a worry or a threat. However, those who had been guests for a while recognized that no physical or emotional threats (other than those which they harbored within their imaginations,) existed on the grounds, and soon they became accustomed to a fairly open and relaxed interaction with both staff and other guests.

Afternoons on Bingo day were usually a lead-up to a stand-off in hysterical behavior. To start with, there was a designated caller, a matron with a high pitched scream for a voice, a lady, named Wanda Lou Gatwick. All who knew her at the facility cautiously referred to her as "Curtains," due to her penchant for wearing what passed for a large purple or magenta "window curtain" gown. She claimed it suited her body type which was just plain large, bordering on huge.

Any Bingo day she called numbers and the rest of the players, typically all ladies, would reiterate the number with some kind of a humorous attachment. It extended the game, gave it a touch of personality, and served to totally confuse any "outsiders" involved. For example, "B-2" became "B-tutu," and hysteria erupted.

Oh yes, the Bingo party was a private club and required some form of initiation, the likes of which only the few select players understood. By some secret decision of the players only ladies were allowed in the Bingo Club. Even then it was a confused state that erupted into mass hysteria as numbers were called out, social comments added, and the gathered multitudes filled the dining hall with shouts, cheers, demands of repeats, and total confusion.

There were never winners in the Bingo hall, rather the event ended in confused hysteria as the "prizes," also called "Bingo Candy" were distributed, blood sugar raced up to 140 plus, and the players departed for other adventures.

There was one additional code adapted by the ladies and applied at some point during a scant few of the games; it was the "Oh Oh!" code.

When the number "O Zero" was called, and was called as "O Zero" things progressed in a normal manner. However, if Curtains decided it was time for excitement, she would call the number as "Oh oh!" and this was a sign that the game was over and with that the mob would dive upon the box of "Bingo Candy" as a lion butchers a limping zebra, and the game was finished, save for the gathering of cards, markers, and the recovery of the exhausted players slumped in corners. Following this action the crowd headed to rooms or the patio. usually to trade candy for cigarettes. Without exception, the same thing was repeated every Bingo day; except for the day after the 'Captain' arrived, to fill in for Gerk.

Gerk had a sister, Ronda, who suffered from a form of selective sight failure and lived in Augsburg, Austria. Ronda lived in a care facility and distressed under the likely misbelief that due to her wealthy status she was above living at the humble estate which Gerk administered, so she lived far away at a rather regal estate for the eccentric and wealthy who were "retired." She rather infrequently communicated with Gerk by telegram, telephone, or mail, when it got through.

Back a few years, during her younger days, she resided at a palatial country estate including two small castles and a workforce of grounds crew, maids, a throng of arthritic butlers, fat cooks, a culinary staff of three sisters and of course, a properly liveried chauffeur on hand to operate her 1936 Rolls Royce Lagatto Salon; an absolutely stunning example of earlier Rolls Royce style and design.

Hard times had failed to visit Ronda, survivor of a long deceased Duke of some wealth and influential extension of the monarchy.

Post war Europe was still in the throes of a badly disrupted, mostly destroyed, and a dual-administered occupied-government communication system, resulting in rail, radio, telephone, and postal systems in total chaos.

Ronda's mail might arrive in weeks after dispatch, and then again it might not arrive at all. The mail which did not arrive posed no problems; after all who missed something they never knew existed to begin with?

Sounded like some of the members of the "stranded in the hallway" crowd at *Goldene Lebensjahre.*

Gerk addressed his office staff, "My administrative assistant, Bert," will be back from his train trip to Denmark and will join us within the week. He will run things here during my absence." Gerk addressed the office staff.

"However, I have selected a name from the pool of office substitutes who qualifies to stand in for me also." He had decided to catch a train to Augsburg and visit with his sister.

"This assistant comes from England and was administrating a sanitarium there during and briefly following war years." He continued. "There is very little about her life since. I suspect she disappeared from the grid same as so many who suffered mentally if not physically damaging effects of The War."

Gerk packed and prepared to take a car to the train station; when a phone call, which he wished had been one of the calls which did not go through, arrived to mash up more of his plans.

He was, if possible, more stressed than ever as he slammed down the phone. "Well, Bert won't join us, not for a while," he informed Winnie and Wilma with stress in his words. "That was a nurse from an Axis hospital in Heidi, Denmark. He was involved in a train accident, the result of a collapsing railroad bridge, blown up by retreating Nazi armies, no doubt."

He pulled an artfully executed Nazi salute and continued a somewhat deteriorated tirade. "He will be in hospital for several weeks; shattered leg." Spoken almost as if Bert was to blame for the ton of failing railroad equipment derailing the car and crushing his leg.

"Call Advair-postings and request the lady… what the heck was her name? Anyway, the 'Captain' they called her I guess. Have her report here as soon as possible, tell her things have changed and we can use her help now, today in fact. I've got to go; will be in contact, assuming some form of contact functions."

Gerk pounced upon his luggage, grappled with the door lever and heaved himself into a waiting car; off to the Bahnhof.

"What the heck is going on here?" Wilma was uneasy over sudden changes, uncomfortable with new collaborators; she who had been with Gerk for thirty-five years.

"Hey, sister not to worry. This 'Captain,' whoever she is, will arrive and do just fine. And remember, we are the foundation here, after all these years who can present a problem?" Thus spoken, Winnie flopped onto a close-at-hand overstuffed entry hall chair, and waited with expectation for the arrival of a part-time administrator.

In a not so subtle presence, I worked at slowly masking the windows in the entry hall in preparation for painting trim, while surreptitiously waiting for the arrival of the 'Captain.'

"Heck, bet 'ya she arrives in a Rolls sporting leather boots and an alligator bag." Wilma was one for dressing up trash just for the sake of ridiculing it later on, in full-blown humor, of course.

"I don't know," Winnie was more uneasy than ever. "There is always opportunity for a crisis. I fear this is as good a foundation as any." She glanced at her sister who was already in positon on the cushions for a snooze. Wilma, somewhat reluctantly joined her,

Within the hour, catching the two dozing, the entry door at *Goldene Lebensjahre,* a massive hulk of timber and heavy glass, was flung open with the force of a hurricane. I was just able to jump aside and rescue a half gallon of a very warm burgundy trim in semi-gloss. Not a good accent blotched on top of light gray carpeting.

"What on earth…"

"All right, so who's next in line, under me that is?" A screech rather than a voice, indicative of many years drinking cheap gin.

Winnie and Wilma, to be truthful, found themselves awakened from a fairly deep afternoon slumber, and were silently stunned. No words came out.

The parrot voice continued, louder if possible. "Where is this Kirk, or Merk, or Gerk person?" A slight pause to recuperate from the exercise of shouting.

This outrageous behavior, was more typically attached to a new guest registering, began to damp down and the next round of barks was just a little above a roar.

"What the heck is this place? Images of a bombed out pig sty come to mind." The female, dressed in a tattered army officer's trench coat and snow-crusted combat boots, pulled off a grubby trilby revealing a filthy mop atop a face calculated to stop an attacking wolf.

No one spoke: fear, confusion, certainly not respect.

"By now you're fully aware that I'm the Captain. I'm in charge. So, now as we have that covered who are my workers? I mean among all of you gapers, like fish-out-of-water. Who the hell works here and what are the rest of you doing out of your cells wandering the halls?"

The wicked witch turned her head my way and with a sort of gasp shouted, "What in the hell do you think you're doing? Huh? Huh?"

She flicked a vulgar gesture my way and said, "Dismissed, go away, you look like some form of filthy scarecrow." Wow, I know I'm skinny but…

"Go on, tell me this isn't happening," Winnie, in a whisper. "This is not the person Gerk appointed, err, and hired to cover for, how long?"

She gazed in terror at the image of a dictator of troops disguised as a filthy army grunt and impersonating an administrator of a care facility.

"Oh not so, tell me…"

Wilma came to the rescue, if only in voice, as she was wedged to her chair in terror of the item addressing the gathered multitudes in the entry hall.

"Oh, a good afternoon to you, Captain." She attempted to display some degree of courtesy, but found it difficult, her voice shaking like a small child about to be admonished for some juvenile crime. "I am Wilma and my sister here is Winnie. We are…"

"I don't give a rat's fanny (she used a freer anatomical term here) who or what you are. Where is my office and what time do they serve drinks around here?"

Just a guess mind you, but I would venture that the 'Captain' had seldom been beyond an arm's reach of a drink's tray for the better part of all her years, amounting to approximately eighty-five from her looks.

"Let me show you to the office and your quarters. Right this way Captain." By the way, what shall we call you, what is your name?" Slight stammer of fear and perhaps a degree of respect, Wilma.

"Shut up and call me Captain, of course. Where is my room and where do I get a drink? I don't hold with this state of inmates wandering all over the place. Take them to their cells and lock the doors. There is no place for such liberation in Sanitariums, not while I'm in command!" Another order belted forth into corridors now filled to overflowing with the silence of fear, anger, perhaps respect, and the groundwork for an explosion. It came, but from an unexpected source.

"Tell you what dear, we're all well behaved and free guests living here." Three cheers for a brave-hearted bingo hall caller. It lasted about as long as it took the Captain to draw another explosive breath.

"Shut up that babbling bird and put her into solitary in the cellar." Back to the shreaking voice now.

"Drive the rest of this rabble to cells and show me my room and, Get. Me. A. Drink!"

No longer a human voice, rather what erupted had escalated into a grotesque shriek.

Wilma and her shaken sister ushered the Captain, whose movements suggested she had already consumed a boatswains' daily stake of hard drink, into Gerk's small quarters and informed her that dinner would be served at five pm sharp. "You will have a choice to eat-in or join our guests in the dining hall." Fat chance that.

"Are you senseless? You apparently are just another, inmate to even consider such insanity. Hell no, I'm not 'dining' with that horde. The maid will serve all my meals here; now **get me a drink**!"

The astonished sisters discussed the next direction to travel, reality or cover.

"She expects to be waited on; well not likely. Who is this monster and where does this leave us? Gerk is gone, a witch in charge and her referring to our guests as inmates and prisoners and calling their rooms cells? And what's with this drink?"

Wilma needed answers and precious few presented themselves.

"Let's get her some port from the kitchen. Heavens knows she looks as if a smidgen of '28 Krug has not visited her pantry in recent times. Bath tub gin more like."

Winnie referred to the ghastly product of the twelve years of American prohibition, typically manufactured in backroom bathtubs and amounting to alcohol and pine oil.

The situation in the front hall had worsened as news of the rude and hostile "Captain" circulated among the guests. Comments flew; some just mouthed according to what others uttered, but some had basement logic.

"Who is she to call us inmates and what's this about being locked in cells?" Curtains had a powerful voice and stood up for resident's rights.

"Is that 'Captain' the item which Gerk left us with? I thought he cared about us..."

"Now Wanda remain calm. The Captain is just overtired after her trip. She'll be fine with a rest and a drink of wine." Good recovery Winnie. "I'm on my way to the kitchen for a glass for her now; then she can rest a bit before dinner."

The Captain was not amused by the glass of weak red fluid and flung it container and all at the wall with a resounding crash, resulting in a light rose splotch on my fresh plaster and paint, and a frightening shout.

"What in the world is this swill? Well? I asked for a drink, not some cooking vinegar or whatever on earth this weak and reeking fluid is." She was trembling, and going quite pale, had broken into a sweat. "Get me a drink or by all the saints I will have you fired along with that poo-faced hag you keep referring to as 'sister.'"

"Winnie, you know that small flask Gerk keeps in his office fridge? Best you get it here quickly." Wilma had bypassed permission; better to ask later for forgiveness.

A restful hour later the Captain was discovered slumped over on the sofa in Gerk's day room, reeking of strong drink and displaying an outstretched hand still clutching the boss's small bottle of Peppermint Schnapps; not surprisingly - empty.

She was emitting a rasping noise, rather like the 6:40 out of Liverpool; when it ran.

"She won't be wanting any dinner." Winnie continued. "Anyway, I'm certainly not going to be the dupe to waken her. And most likely she would not like our meatloaf anyway."

From out in the hall I shuddered at the thought, and applied my brush to smooth crimson trim. Wilma headed out to call for dinner and encourage the multitudes to the dining hall.

"Shall we lock her door?" A grin akin to that of a schoolboy was added as an admonishment, and so they locked it. "Safe for a while, but then what?"

Out in the hall I broke into silent applause for the brave sisters.

Dinner complete, many guests retired to the radio room, bedrooms, or to sitting in the halls with light conversation being exchanged. It was a typical evening.

Curtains was entertaining a few members of the Bingo Club with her imitation of the already notably rancorous Captain. Meanwhile, *Sticks* discovered a new route from the front door to the laundry via a storage closet which he discovered could be unlocked with the aid of a small putty knife "pinched" from my paint cart; his mobility was momentarily safer from "them blasted beaches."

Sticks was getting the upper hand over his foes at last! The Captain had been put away for the evening and by morning things might just have improved.

During the night, while the Captain slept off a fair portion of a half-liter of schnapps, the guests wandered, slept some, visited in the halls, and slept some more.

The staff made rounds and copied notes into logs.

Outside, snow fell far thicker than normal, and by dawn it was obvious no one would be spending time outdoors; not painters, not walkers, neither Teddy or Myrtle. There was a small gazebo in a back patio and it collected a frantic and limited band of those who braved the elements to enjoy a rushed smoke. Everyone else spent the day, other than meals, in rooms, hallways (so much for progress in plaster and paint,) the two radio rooms, a relaxed reading room complete with comfortable chairs and a fireplace, and two day-rooms. Gerk had furnished the place with two elderly pianos, a fair-sized library, and four ping pong tables for the guest's enjoyment. It looked to be a long winter's day, and then the Captain erupted from her chamber with the explosive poise of a bull moose during rutt, and everything pretty much went to pieces.

"I want everyone in the dining room now!" She was not about to let it be done with one command, "Now, Now, Now, I want every one of you inmates in there *right now!*"

Edson, right on cue, burst through the door, and wheeled across the dining room and slammed into the Captain. "Waaaa Waaaa secrets, I've got secrets!"

Most everyone, upon reconsideration, would agree that this was most likely the event which set things rolling, or boiling, or exploding. Anyway, the Captain went berserk and, climbing onto one of the dining tables, detonated into wild gestures and hysterical screaming, "Get everyone in here, now!"

Winnie and Wilma raced from room to room with one plan in mind, that of keeping the Captain calm. Wilma was shaking and hardly able to speak without a stutter. "She…She's insane, still dru…drunk and gone right over the edge. God help us all if she has a gun or knife."

Wilma and her sister arrived at the same conclusion, no good would come from searching all the rooms as several guests were missing; perhaps hiding, smoking outside, just in the restrooms, or visiting other rooms and unaware of the call to the dining area.

"We've got to get back there." Winnie took command. "Heaven knows what's that crazy person is capable of doing to our family."

I was in between the entry and the front dining room at the time, attacking paint and plaster, while plotting the attack on the Captain, should it become necessary. I also was anxious for the safety of Gerk's residents and workforce. There was not another male staff member on duty.

Screams from the dining area answered that question, and fortified the dread in the sisters as they accelerated into a run, down hallways, (breaking all rules about running in the halls,) and around corners into the dining room, just as the Captain emerged and shrieked orders into the hallway for the "inmates" to obey her and "Get your arses in here right now." This incised Karley who, standing by the door grabbed the Captain by the wrist and gave it a good horse-strength bite.

"Ahhhh you little monster!"

Karley nipped into a nearby restroom, only to be replaced by *Teddy* on the run. He held his arm high and in a charm never before seen, tossed his 'wife' (filled with some form of hot beverage) across the hallway to *Myrtle*, who caught the cherished drinking vessel, and rammed it down on the Captain's head; forever smashing the *Wedgewood-Wife*. This furthered the cause and resulted in countless shrieks from the Captain. This was all followed by a most charitable act as *Myrtle* and *Teddy* then joined hands and charged the Captain in an all-out stampede aimed at dropping her not unlike some college rugby scrimmage. Their ploy was only bested by *Sticks* who emerged from his newly-discovered corner in the laundry, arms full of wet table cloths fresh from the wash in which he smothered the Captain. *Freda Ryan*, in a true act of charity, slammed her best Easter lampshade onto the Captain's head, resulting in a well-wrapped and blinded Captain. Further brilliance followed as *Sticks* returned with his "treasure," a large rubber alligator, which he slammed directly into the face of the already fairly disoriented Captain rendering her as harmless as, "Them darned beaches under my bed!" In a blinded withdrawal, the 'Captain' plodded across the hall, and with a most ungraceful entry landed with both feet into my tub of wet plaster. She cursed and attempted to slog away but at that moment Wanda Lou Gatwick gave out with the ultimate Bingo call, "Oh Oh!" and the charge to the Bingo Candy Canister on the center table in the dining hall safely emptied the hallway crowd to one very outraged, bundled, blinded, and hobbled Captain, plus two slightly drained sisters of mercy.

Ultimately the telephone disbursed the Politzei from a nearby berg, who arrived in record time and were happy to deliver the Captain, sporting hardened plaster boots, a layer of soggy table cloths, a gauche pink lampshade and still thrashing and fighting, to a very cold and dank jailhouse cell. A fitting venue for the Captain, who was more the likes of a World War II Nazi Officer.

"Whatever will we tell Gerk?" Wilma was worried.

"Hell, tell him the Captain got plastered in the hall!"

The two, in fits of laughter dropped into hallway chairs, leaned back in relaxed repose, and made very nice creases in my fresh plaster.

Now, who was in for a plastering?

A WANDERER'S GUIDE TO GOD

F ully aware of what I was letting myself in for that morning, sometime around the 20th century, I set off in quest of a fresh donut and inadvertently ran into God.

Oh, it didn't occur all at once like – rather it was spread over a nomadic lifetime quest.

Alpine trails submitted to my ambitious boot prints and long patches of asphalt fell beneath compressed-bike tires.

The ice fields of a remote U.S. Navy intercept site atop some Aleutian Island, slid on a ruckus trail to tidal waves off Zuma Beach, 'neath my slippery surfboard as my tanned hide became salted from hours on beaches searching for some anxious lady with a bent on wandering, love and waves.

Ages of redundant bla bla, in endless tedium, struck a slightly distorted note to my flight through intellectual institutions; many semesters of class hours, later I was released to penal servitude amidst acres of education-bored school kids; leaving a smile of content for a half-century stretch in institutions of learning.

United above 10,000 feet with St. Mary's Pass, into lush pines and granite outcroppings, her sifted trails accepted my dusty and well-worn boots, my water filter, and a grin, then released to me sights, smells and blessed silence as my stove proffered up countless mugs of Foo-Foo, numerous pots of soup, ample allocations of stew and piles of pop-over Shepard's pies.

Another trail trodden 'neath exhausted boots, further snowbound tent sites, a leg-tired pull up endlessly steep roads with ultra-light frame atop spent bike tires, and chapter 73 of my life's quest edged me closer to God, mercifully closer.

But I still haven't found that blasted donut!

MAXINE

I t had been my mistake from the onset. I mean, the second I saw her I assumed that she was a vagrant, perhaps a bum, maybe homeless. To my rather untrained eye everything pointed that way.

She was sitting, slightly slumped against her filthy tow-sack on the rear porch of the education department office; certainly not the typical roost for drifters just off the main streets of Riverdale, California. Other clues to her itinerant nature were the fact that she was perched, in a clearly unladylike manner, cross legged on a greasy back dock in an alley.

Her old baggie stockings were rolled half way down flabby thighs displaying undesirable glimpses into fields of plump white flesh, much of which I suspect had not seen the light of day for longer than one should be forced to guess.

Meanwhile, tucked surreptitiously into her waistband was what appeared to be a half pint of the hard stuff wrapped in a paper sack and displaying through a jagged hole in the sack, a remaining half of the good-times brown liquid.

Clutched in her arthritic left claw, in a rather theatrical gesture, she flourished the smoldering butt of her most recent smoke. Demonstrating much practiced flicks of a crusty wrist (a wrist which had certainly spent a lifetime without a woman's Rolex), she dredged from the burlap tow-sack, a stained and well rumpled pack of hard-core, non-filtered smokes and stuffed yet another into her saggy mug. There it perched, stuck to chapped and wrinkled lips as she administered to it the smoldering end of the old dying smoke and lit the new one.

Her hands, so dark stained, could mistakenly identify her as a field worker in the midst of the walnut harvest. However, it wasn't walnut oil which had turned her primeval fingers brown, rather the nicotine residue from many years of indulging in the non-stop smoking of non-filtered cigarettes.

A frenzied cough, the result of yet another lung-killing inhalation of tobacco smoke, shook first her hand then her entire body. Sputum flew from her frantic lips as she coughed again and again; the remains of her breathing passages reminding her dying lungs that time was running out for this chain smoker.

A closet alcoholic and chain smoker, the single scrap missing from this *Rockwell* slice of Americana, was a filthy mouth mixed with nose picking and spitting. She did not let me down on all three.

"What the devil you staring at anyway?"

She glared at me with a killer snarl.

"And what ya' want here?" She addressed me with a raspy voice, deepened by years of cheap gin would be my guess. "Can't a girl enjoy her break, a few seconds off from your sneering mug and away from my crappy basement job?"

This item had not been a "girl" for well over sixty years. She turned a knotted neck and indicated a dark stairway down. "I gotta sit down 'n that pit through the same dogma day in and day out."

She ended the tirade with a good one handed nostril blowing onto the very sack she carried her trash in. She uttered an oath with words which would have made most sailors and all truck drivers blush. What remained lodged within the vented nostril she pried out with a crusty unvarnished nail - and flung my way! Then continued with her much practiced dressing down.

"You, boy," still directed my way, "take your baby face and fancy dress around to the front door and let them deal with whatever's brought you to this part of my already crappy day, and leave me the heck alone."

She dismissed me off with the flip of a hairy, filthy wrist, and she graced me with, "Scat, white collared do-gooder!"

Nothing in my rather sheltered life as a school teacher had prepared me for the disgusting encounter in the alley with the offensive item that would become known to me as Maxine. (Although her real name, according to a 50 year-old social security card, discovered on her person after her untimely death by drowning, was Mary-Alice Cardiff.)

During her break on the back dock behind the office building, Maxine eyed the disease and vermin of the alley with a most practiced distain, a capacity she filled with admiration. Inside the building at her job she dished out a totally different form of malice.

She was actually an under-secretary to the district superintendent of education, and the only person alive privy to the use of the much hated school-district attendance-grading system.

The system had been done away with years ago, (to the euphoric delight of all who had taught elementary school in the district.) It had been replaced with a painlessly efficient computerized system of monitoring the budding scholars in the K through 8th grades. Then, around the turn of the century some fanatical person with a bent on the cruel and malicious, reinstated the dreadful old system.

Outraged teachers throughout the district ran amuck, departed for unskilled work in Sri Lanka or retired early. The report from the district, "Don't like it? Well guess what? Now you gotta do both systems!"

Maxine was housed, for lack of a better word, in a small chamber in the sub-basement, deep in the bowels of the old stone and mortar office building, site of the district education center. Her "office" was the now inoperable boiler room for the steam power plant which once heated the colossal old three-story building. The chamber still held numerous pipes, valves and a portion of an immense water tank, part of the steam generation system. The remainder of which had been replaced by a much advanced gas-electric system.

Her duties at work were quite simple: keep correcting and returning the attendance and grade books. Errors or not, keep them on the move. And indeed they moved.

Daily, books arrived in a steady stream from hysterically concerned and overworked teachers. Maxine went over them, rejected them, and they made their dawdling way back to infuriated teachers all over the Riverdale area.

All that was necessary for the final demise of dear Maxine would have been for her to pass back the books without a single error to correct. She was not about to let that happen. She had been working at her job for fifty-two years and loved to inflict pain. She visualized those teachers upon receipt of their corrected books as they sat, squirmed, and screamed loudly. "NO, not more corrections!"

Her technique of indicating the needed corrections was not unlike that of a machine gun dispelling yellow sticky notes and red pencil slashes per page.

It was only seconded by suspiciously slopped brown liquid, burnt cigarette holes and frayed edges of the books as they withstood her scrutiny and disgusting social habits. They left the place as smoldering wreckage on its way back to aghast teachers for yet more corrections. The system was a closed-ended *Catch-22*, never-ending-nightmare of redundancy.

I went around to the entrance on Main Street, a turn-of-the-century storefront, albeit comfortably more inviting than the alley occupied by the nasty item that I selected to remember as a witch without a pointed hat. I checked my composure and walked inside, somewhat reluctantly.

My original meaning for the visit was to discuss with the person who scored the record books from the dark place, the exact reason, if reason there be, for all the corrections being made; corrections to information about which no one could possibly know enough to judge whether right or wrong.

I stated my name, my school location and my business. I waited. It hit!

"Are you confused? I mean, are you completely lost in your thinking?"

I was aghast. My question had been straight forward, well founded, and certainly stated politely. What had gone wrong with my day? I had been torpedoed twice now and was on the very edge of exploding.

"I'm so sorry," almost sarcastically. "But, what are you talking about?" I addressed a simple looking soul, dressed more or less like a peasant and having the facial characteristics of one who could be considered mentally dawdling. (Parentage related at birth, and all that.)

She answered my question with a question; yet further indication of one with not quite everything functioning properly. "What do you want here? Are you looking for a public restroom? Well, we don't have one. You best go down the street, find a gas station or use the park."

Did she mean use the bushes in the park, or was there an available public restroom there for people off the street; people like me, I guessed. Suddenly the roles were switched, the lady (sic) in the alley was at home there and I was the one who was a homelessly lost soul. I felt ill and wanted to leave.

Staff back at my school were depending on my return bearing information dealing with the *record book crisis*. I could not let them down. I tried again.

"Perhaps you can direct me toward the lady who corrects the attendance and grade books." I attempted to ignore the fact that she also had crooked glasses, the start of a moustache, and wore her hair just exactly as it had been when she erupted following her nocturnal recline under whatever rock she had spent the night.

"I need some information for my school staff and thought I would ask the person who would be best informed, that would be someone named Maxine who corrects the books." I paused to let it all ooze in, figuring that too much information might confuse her.

"Uh, Maxine? You want to talk with Maxine?" She sounded almost on the verge of laughter. "Well, ok, you can sure have some fun with that one. Ha, ha, ha, ha, ha!" The volume escalated to a triple fortissimo crescendo, bordering on a frightening hysterical level.

I looked around me to determine if I had in fact entered the wrong doorway, and was in some form of psycho ward. Nope, the sign on the door said Education Administrative Office. I was in the right place. She however, had perhaps missed the boat and arrived here by accident. I gave up on gaining information and just said, "Show me the way to Maxine." I added, "Now!" The slow often respond best to commands. It worked.

"Well, don't have to be rude." She glared at me. "Take the stairs over there," she indicated a dark corridor downward, "and just keep on going. Her room is below the basement and there sure won't be much light." Grin. "Hope you ain't 'fraid of the dark."

I feared less the dark and more what I might discover looming down there in the darkness. I walked to the murky corridor, and began the trek downward. She was right on both scores; it was dark, and it was a long way down too.

In the darkness I stumbled, and almost bashed my head on the steel of a large doorframe looming in the darkness. The air had become damp and earthy, the smell not unlike dirt just turned over; a grave crossed my mind. There was also a powerful smell of something burning. My mind flashed back briefly to my years in the U. S. Navy and a most dismal and forlorn job in a burning chamber on the island of Adak.

I regained my composure, along with my footing, and reached a steel chamber door. Just visible in the gloom and dankness of the basement corridor, an old and faded sign on the door read:

Boiler Room - Danger

However, someone with the handwriting of a four year old had scratched letters over it which read:

Corrections- Stay Out

I knocked and waited. The place was gruesome and I wanted to be gone. What on earth was this? I had come to discuss school work and ended up a character in an Edgar Allen Poe story.

I knocked again, this time rather loudly I guessed, but I was all for getting my business done and regaining the freedom of daylight.

"What in the hell do you want?" The voice screamed out from inside the door and the echo hung in the cold and damp air far too long.

I grasped the lever on the hatch, reminders of shipboard fittings, and shoved inward. The stench within almost made me vomit on the floor.

Within it was darker, dismal, filthy, stunk like a bad sewer connection. Sitting in the midst of the nasty mess of piled papers, papers, papers, papers everywhere, squatting beside a crusty mattress covered with the filth only associated with the squatters found in riverside homeless camps, squatting there and relieving herself into a grossly-overflowing rusty bucket was…Maxine!

I had tolerated just enough. That was altogether too much for anyone to stand, and I pulled fast the door, turned and raced along the mossy and leaking corridor to the stairs up. The door at the top of the stairs was open, and the best description of my exit was 'eruption.' I was blown outward and into daylight, landed at a jog and reached the corner and my parked car at a fast run.

Nothing on earth would take me back there to that terrible sight and smell. No duty to my school or to my organization could encourage me to return even a phone call. I assessed the situation and ruled on the side of hygiene over loss and removed my shoes and tossed them into the gutter prior to entering my vehicle.

I arrived back at my school late in the afternoon, turned in my room keys, filled out an emergency leave request and drove home.

After a long night of heavy drinking and light thinking and a conversation with the wall and my conscience, I drove to work the following afternoon and submitted my resignation. I was done. Finished. Washed up. No more school, no more little nippers, and no more blasted attendance and record books from the dark side!

There was considerable confusion the following day at the Education Department office on Main Street in Riverdale. It was obvious that there had been a death; exactly who and how was slightly less obvious and only sometime later would the facts come together.

Upon the startling experience of seeing Edger Weiss enter her secretive chamber in the subbasement, Maxine went slightly nuts. Seems she was expecting a plumber to help to unstop her disgustingly plugged bathroom drain, and she was ill prepared for the features of the same man she had verbally accosted in the alley to darken her doorway. Upon that realization she thrashed about, knocked over a massive stack of well overdue attendance and record books amounting to several years back work, and piled about six feet high by a good three feet wide. The pile overbalanced and fell on her, causing her to stumble and wedge her foot in the chamber pot. She had time to utter one final curse as she slipped on the disgusting spilled refuse awash on the floor. Upon falling downward, her head contacted the brass control valve on the massive old steam boiler water supply tank and knocked it off.

Under pressure about seven hundred gallons of old stagnant water erupted out through the three-inch fitting and in short time her small chamber was filled well above waist depth.

The unconscious body of Maxine remained submerged, and gradually she inhaled enough water to overcome her dying lungs and she did in fact succumb.

The silence in the dank cellar that day was only seconded by the silence at her memorial, which was attended by two stray dogs, a drunk who happened along, and knowing Maxine rather well, decided it might be a good time to pinch her bottle. Unfortunately for him it had become lost in the flood and he left the event dry. The only other person to attend was a Mrs. K. from a local school, who arrived out of curiosity, and left with a wide grin and a cheer on her lips.

Seems she had been accused of failure to complete corrections to seventeen years of back work in the attendance and record books, all of which had become lost in the basement flood. All agreed with her parting shot, "Stuff the ol' bag! We're finally done with those blasted books of terror!"

The following month, the Education Department went back to the computer program, but rumor has it that someone in Riverdale is experimenting with the discovered remains of a single copy of those ancient attendance and record books belonging to someone named Weiss, and is considering a revised form of the spiteful system. Word has it the new proram could hit the schools in spring 2023!

STREETS PAVED IN BLOODY GOLD

Preface

Women, young and old, both horrified and tolerant, clustered in moderately-hushed groups, as well as isolated individuals erupting into rampant hysteria and distress. Men also joined in the grieving and crying as all lined the muddy street on that tearfully winter-clogged morning. Huddled, all in misery, over the portions of bled-out bodies piled like so much log-wood. Downcast eyes wept tears and reluctant hands pawed through the ghastly remains in agonizing hope of identifying relatives and friends. Meanwhile, the sagging-board sidewalks held their creaking tongues, rendering not a clue to what had lent so ghastly a tone to any Sunday's morning visage. The slush-chilled dawn harbored what in a better time may have passed for clothing, boots, saddle bags, and one size seven Stetson reluctantly revealing a crimson-rimmed hole through the filthy sweat-stained crown. No comfort and precious little peace solaced the degrees of frost, emotional or atmospheric on that December morning: Columbia, California, gold country, 1850.

History

Within months of March 24th of 1850, following the discovery of gold in a small spring-fed stream close to the settlement of Columbia, California, there were tents, board shacks, even caves housing thousands of optimistic miners with picks, shovels, cradles, and minds as well as arms, engaged in the struggle to find, claim, and excavate from mother earth's reluctant face the precious twenty dollars per ounce "color" known as… "GOLD!

Arrival

I sailed from the Seattle steamship docks, with a sagging rucksack loaded down with hope, some well-worn clothing, scant few tools of my trade, and a sacred document vested upon me by *Mc Gill College* in Canada. I was a newly licensed medical doctor, green as the Pacific waves thrown aside by the bow of our ancient ship as we steamed toward our destination of San Francisco, California.

Three cold and seasick weeks later, on a dreary Thanksgiving Day of that year, we touched the San Francisco docks onboard the overcrowded and rapidly rusting hulk misnamed *Queen of the Oceans.* I was extremely thankful for surviving the sea voyage, but as a member of the "new gold prospector" crowd, I was still green; green as the forests I trudged through on my journey forever northward.

Although I had grown up in northern Canada, miles of hiking later, I discovered myself to be more than just a little unprepared for such harsh conditions of cold and hunger, I plodded the journey's final mile through wet muddy masses of frantically working miners. I had arrived in California's gold-wild settlement of Columbia, and a less enchanted and forlorn huddled mass of thrown-together and rough-built structures, shacks and hovels, (individuals included), I would be hard-pressed to find.

However, luck prevailed and my eyes discovered two dimly-flickering kerosene lanterns swinging in the cold evening's wind outside

Sally's Kitchen, and once inside those sagging timber doors, I realized a haven of warmth, light, a degree of comfort, and…hot food.

The place was liberally heated by two huge iron stoves glowing cherry-red from opposite corners of the timber room; one in use for cooking what turned out to be delicious hot food, the other served as a source of heat, and apparently as a site to dry stinking and steaming items of clothing, suspended from ropes strung about the area. The whole remainder of the room was crowded with coarse wood benches swarming around rickety tables, all overflowing with greasy dishes, half-eaten food, muddy rucksacks, and men's exhausted arms. All of this, plus the smoky hot atmosphere of a full blown cooking kitchen, steaming clothing dryer, elevated voices approaching a shout, an out-of-tune player-piano belting out backeast show tunes, and the bang and clatter of utensils; all of this and yet I felt some degree of peace and well-being in my new surroundings.

Setting

The following morning saw me refreshed from a hot indoor bath, rested from an expensive night in a room over *"Sally's,"* nourished from a sit-down breakfast, including bacon, four eggs, homemade biscuits, and …real hot coffee served in a cup. Only after all of this luxury did I take the time to be anxious, as the town's new medical doctor, anxious to meet my sponsor.

D.O. Miles, dressed like the rich entrepreneur and banker that he was, met me at the door to his substantial brick and iron office building. He ushered me, rather quickly, directly into a room which would have done justice to an east coast house of prostitution. One of four banks in the town of 5000 inhabitants, this one seemed an out-of-character facility. Situated in a rough, muddy, mountainside community, it revealed walls papered in scarlet and accented with settings bedizened in gold and red, tables displaying tinsel-garland lamps, and lastly the entire two offices were furnished in well-worn red leather furniture. The atmosphere, equally overwhelming, harbored a pungent cigar smoke and furniture polish patina. It was a true San Francisco style bank building standing four square in the mud deep Sierra foot hills of gold-hungry Columbia.

"Scanlon," Miles came right to the point. "I'm a man of few words and believe in setting the plan out for you without a lot of cover up and hemming and hawing."

Short, going to a potbelly, sporting the savage side-whiskers of the time, and in a tailed coat too small for his motivated paunch, D.O. was on a mission and was not wasting time listening to me discuss the fact that he was a banker and I was a medical doctor.

Slight and tall, sporting skin darkened by hours in the sun, as well as my heritage of French-Canadian, I was a full 6 inches taller than D.O. and a couple of stones lighter.

"I thank you for sponsoring me sir, and hope I can repay you in my medical practice in the community." I said what I wanted to establish and dressed it with what I suspect he wanted to hear as well.

"I recall you mentioned a small, empty building, with a space to practice medicine, as well as a room for sleeping and reading."

I glanced at Miles and continued. "I'm willing to frequent local eateries for nutritious meals, returning business to the community for their supporting my medical practice."

I paused to check what appeared to be a loss of focus. Was I going too fast, too slow; maybe getting the cart ahead of the horse…somehow I felt I had drifted off course, had lost touch with D.O.

"Err, does this sound like what you requested from me in our last correspondence before I set sail from Seattle?"

D.O. had left the room. I mean, he was totally gone mentally. Shortly I realized, he was snoring and was passing off powerful exhaust fumes of alcohol. Barely ten in the morning and the pillar of the economic scene in the community was - drunk!

Plotting

The two Calvin brothers joined an irate Po Lim for some midday food and drink in the damp *Mine Shack* eatery, just uphill and yet a far cry from *Sally's*. The rough board dump was only slightly warmed by an inadequate smoldering fireplace and smelled of smoke, old beer, and earth. The three slumped at a table, as they planned the gold robbery from the bank and water company offices of Mr. D.O. Miles. They lived in a desperate dirt and rock cave outside of Columbia and most of what they possessed was the result of robbery, swindling, corruption, and gambling.

The brothers, Homer with a wooden leg, and Hal with only one eye, bore deformities subsequent to crimes against other miners, which left them crippled, fuming, and vengeful.

They had only recently arrived in Columbia, straight out of the Sonora Jail, having served a single year for a knife assault on a stage driver during a robbery. The driver died, the shotgun guard eventually succumbed to his wounds; wounds received defending the passengers who, under question, were unable to recall exactly who had done the killing. (Passengers it was later disclosed, had been 'rewarded' twenty dollars each for their silence.) The charges against the brothers were "Using a deadly weapon during the robbery of federal funds." The strongbox on the stage contained newly minted coins from the San Francisco Federal Mint, thus making the crime a felony.

Po Lim was in no mood to listen to any drivel from the two jailbirds. "You both shut up and listen. We're doing this job my way. I've had enough of the law and stupid partners to last me forever."

Po Lim had a history of committing heinous crimes including murder, decapitation, robbery, and destruction of wagon trains. He was so used to killing by this time that another death was totally meaningless to him.

"Get over any thought of getting ahead of me and scampering with the gold. I will search you out and kill you one by each!"

He stopped to pull on a bottle of cheap whiskey, stolen from the backroom shelf at the local grocery while the clerk was busy in the front, cleaning up the mess his two partners had made to cover the theft. His escape out the back door meant very little to his way of thinking; just another, robbery of such trivial items as the bottle, two slabs of bacon, and some canned goods. Po seldom considered consequences of punishment; just kill whoever was unfortunate enough to be there in his way.

"I have two small bags of black powder I stole while working on some wagon road cuts outside of Jamestown." He thought back to other painful times, both physical and emotional, of hard rock aqueduct work and the inevitable robbery from the site.

"There was that rotten bunch working on ditches out of Fuller's Crossing too. Blasted white man's country; them paid almost twice what the Chinese received."

He declined to discuss another use of his stash of black powder, a chain of atrocious crimes gone bad a couple of years back involving both *The 21 Mile House* and *The Long Barn Lodge*, mountain lodgings located up the pass from Colombia.

"We will make use some of this 'magic black powder' to open back wall of D.O.'s bank." He gave forth a filthy, gap-toothed grin at his own lame humor. "Open up, like blow the whole place to hell and take gold from white banker; banker-crook dressed elegant to fool bad-luck miners in this dirt-dump."

He was done, and tossed a small pinch of black powder into the dying fire. 'Boom!' Po smirked, "See what we can do with two bags of this? Come on, let's take a dark look at that bank wall. It's out back, by a rocky crumbling hill, like the top some old cave. No one will care if they see us digging around in dark of night for scraps tossed outback of that crappy Chinese café owned by Wing Pong."

Po made a rude gesture with his hand. "His food stink. He no real Chinese, maybe from Japan." Po spit on the ground to emphasize his feelings and the three walked out into a darkening night of gathering cold.

Sierra country winters were not kind to weakness of any sort, and while Po acknowledged the cold, he considered it shame, or pain, all forms of weakness, to be ignored as "weakness of the white man."

The three men arrived backside of the twin brick buildings: the bank and the water company offices, armed with a rusty shovel, stolen along the way. Homer and Hal commenced to do some digging in the specified areas outside the back walls, holes for placement of small bags of Po's 'magic powder.'

Meanwhile, Po excused himself from the digging, walked a few steps and broke in the back door of the banking office. "Not hard for me break in, the white puts too much trust in a metal door and a big ugly lock." Po spit again, his typical sign of disrespect and laughed at what he considered useless security. "I break into doors all the time; good way get food, clothes, and sometimes money."

He fumbled around in the dark until fire from a sulphur match and a kerosene lantern joined forces to displace some bitter-cold darkness.

"What...?"

His glance into the dark behind him, a darkness which rendered no evidence of what awaited, and exactly as he set down his flickering lantern the steel weapon hit the back of his head; hit with enough impact to fell him into the lantern, which shattered, spilling it's supply of fuel onto the small pile of shotgun shells.

The resulting explosion was powerful enough to kill Po instantly and shatter nearby windows. It straightaway killed the person who bashed Po's brains, and set off the three ensuing explosions, quickly shattering doors, walls, beams, and igniting a fire fierce enough to spread to connecting buildings.

During that half hour the fire consumed major portions of all five buildings; a fire blistering enough to melt brackets on iron door frames and fuse shut steel doors on the bank vaults. Vaults, which upon later examination were found to be void of any contents. The sheriff's ensuing investigation revealed that at the time of the explosion the vaults were both...empty!

Encounter

Within a week I was settled into a small three room cabin on State Street in Colombia with a shingle out front indicating that:

Scanlon De Graf M.D.

had set up practice and was open for customers.

And they came, mostly with old paper bills, and some with gold dust, which required a walk across the street to the assay office, to exchange the twenty dollars in gold for coins or paper. I soon was familiar with the injuries of beat up gold miners, kids with injuries sustained in falls, fights, and digging accidents, and women with scrapes, cuts, and lonesome for a young single man with copper hair and ruddy skin. I dealt with them all, collected payment from about half, and was promised repayment from the remainder. Often payment came in the form of a warm dinner at fireside with a family in Columbia; not something to be taken lightly.

The evening of my fourth day of work found me back at Sally's, with a hunger for home cooked food, and an eye out for a young lady named Charlotte, who had visited my office earlier applying for my advertised assistant's job.

"Good evening doctor," she sat right down, ordered coffee and soup, and addressed me without a degree of bashful reluctance; a tall, well-dressed lady of some worldliness I would suspect.

"May I call you Scanlon," some steel in the voice, "and do you always blush when women address you?"

There she was, halfway into an introduction and I laughed well into my reply, "Yes, and yes."

Charlotte introduced herself and gave me a concise history of the past few months of her life and work explaining that, "I have worked of late as a bookkeeper in the port city of Stockton."

We discussed her work there at the Stockton Gold and Silver Banking Company. She gave me a reference name which I filed.

"Why do you feel qualified to work for me, a licensed medical doctor?" I was not being forthright, rather concerned that the counting of money did not hold with the challenges of nursing the roughness of the dirt and rock miners in Columbia.

"Prior to working in Stockton, I had been a nurse for a while in a small gold rush town in Nevada."

I questioned exactly where, realizing that as a newcomer to California, it would quite possibly not mean much.

"Fuller's Crossing."

Fog. A foreign language. Nothing. I was totally lost, and gathered that almost anything she told me from that point could be information fabricated to pad her way into a job.

"I worked there for a street doctor; worked for about one year, worked until the cold, the mud and snow, and the abusive lifestyle finished me off. During that year we helped the poor and homeless dregs of society. I learned what medicine I know the hard way, including knives, guns, clubs, fists, and all form of foul play, vile street life, and gutter disease. I had to work with every sort of patient, including the Chinese who drifted down river from the Sierra aqueducts and high mountain dam and railroad construction sites."

At this point her voice, as well as her posture, displayed a considerate disdain for those men who suffered no more or less than any who had worked the harsh and dangerous struggle to drive flumes through solid granite in freezing snow and broiling heat. The Chinese laborers had worked for less pay than the whites and sustained just as many injuries in the rough granite. Injuries from explosions and falls. Most had a poor attitude toward whites of any sort, medical doctor or just the common refuse from the streets. I suspected the feelings were mutually displayed.

"I dealt with it all, and one day it was just too much and I bought a seat on the stage headed for the valley and Stockton."

She returned to her meal, finishing off a hefty bowl of thick beef soup and then, sipping her coffee and giving me a hard look, settled into her chair, calmly, while I was somehow expecting conflict. None was offered and we discussed what her job might involve. I asked her medical questions; her answers were in keeping with those I would expect from a candidate with her experience.

"Are you willing to start work tomorrow at nine am," I asked, and I suggested a fee. Following her consideration, and with a settlement on the table, she accepted the terms, finished her coffee, and wished me a good night with an agreement to arrive next morning, at 9 o'clock.

I sat for a while consulting my notes subsequent to the interview, and was satisfied with her answers, with the exception of her reaction to comments concerning the Chinese with whom she had worked. I paid my bill and shrugged my arms into my padded coat, jammed my knit hat down almost to my collar, and hesitantly departed into harsh conditions to match those of the far north.

The night promised to be freezing, and so against the gathering cold and darkness, I trudged home to light a lantern, kindle a robust fire in my hungry iron stove, and heated up water. A book from the tiny local library, a mug of steaming hot coffee, and a wedge of apple pie left from dinner, and I was in for the night.

Meanwhile, outside the temperature continued to fall. I was from Canada and while quite used to winter, this night required a whole lot of firewood, and an extra blanket, or even two. Later, rolled up in my bed, I dozed off sometime before midnight.

Charlotte

While Charlotte worked side by side with me in the simple medical practice I offered, she never opened up with anything save her explanation of facts and experiences in Fuller's Crossing, and very little of that. I suspected she was hiding from a romance gone badly, separation from a loved one, or perhaps she just did not enjoy conversation. Anyway, days passed. We were into the third week together, and yet I felt like I knew as little about Charlotte as I had upon our first meeting.

I was aware of an attitude of somewhat disdain, or perhaps just indifference, Charlotte exhibited toward the Chinese patients who came to the office. I was alert for any display of preference or prejudice, but saw only a slight lack of passion in her presentation toward them. While it was a worry, it never seemed to interfere with the quality of care, which I required. However, this being said, I had to concede that her nursing skills were as good as what I had in mind when I hired her, and in all fairness, her social graces had little bearing upon her job qualification.

One morning she announced that her sister had come to visit and her whole attitude seemed to improve. Perhaps I had been correct that she was just lonesome for someone she missed from back home, and, while she had seldom discussed her sister, none-the-less she did seem to have a renewed interest in everything.

Explosion

My dwelling, a small cabin actually, woke me as it did a somewhat lopsided dance and tossed me, the book and the scant remains of my cup onto the floor. The fire, still burning, although mostly ash and coals, lingered inside the iron stove which did its best to remain upright and attached to the ceiling pipe.

I grabbed my medical bag, heavy coat and hat, and ran into the street. There was no doubt about it, I was not alone in my mad scramble outside into the cold night, nighttime, yet well-lit by what at first appeared to be a forest fire.

As I ran across two streets and between a couple of buildings it was obviously not a forest fire, but a building fire. More so, a town fire, as on count it appeared to be that portions of five buildings were ablaze in such violent eruptions. It put me in mind of the historic English Parliament Building explosion, a revolutionary event celebrated in England and some parts of Canada known as *Guy Fawkes Day*.

The whole town was on the move; kids, women, men, some still dressed in the mud of the mines, some dressed fresh out of bed and only slightly aghast upon discovering they were in night gowns and long underwear.

Stone constructed and iron-reinforced walls, once the backside of the D.O. Miles Bank and Water Company offices, were blown outward by what was determined to be the first explosion, followed closely by a massive landslide of timber, stone, and iron doors approximating a scene from a war.

Frantic witnesses remembered a second and third blast, followed by one massive final explosion which ripped open the backside of other buildings, as well as opening up the ground for about 100 feet in all directions. This information was reported by witnesses, mostly as reliable as the morning stage from Sonora, however each did agree that the largest explosion came from outside the buildings.

These final explosions demolished whatever the initial explosion left standing: a neighboring hillside storage facility, the scant remains of the bank and water company buildings, the East China Café, Bollington's Iron Foundry, and one side of the Silver Bell Saloon. Unfortunate late night workers, inside those buildings, as well as occupants asleep in coldly uncomfortable lofts above, died instantly, or were consumed in the subsequent fires, leaving behind scant ash for identification.

The fire brigade brought into service their newly purchased steam-powered pumper, and gathered whatever auxiliary men and equipment were at hand, and raced the two blocks to the scene.

Little endured for the workers to save or rescue; explosion, avalanche and fire had consumed everything except stone and iron which remained in a uselessly mute slump against mounded refuse, smoldering ashes, and dead, dead, dead.

Morning

A bleak and shocking dawn found the gutters awash in a filthy display of scraps gathered in darkness of so dreary a night, and mounded into the not soon-forgotten nightmare of dawn's frozen harshness.

Assembled into baskets by volunteers, friends, and mourners, was debris from the past night's explosion, debris from fire, screams, and death. Debris included clothing, livery, bodies, and parts of bodies. Debris of less import included, iron, stone, and portions of equipment, supplies, and sundry items of the unfortunate business taken down to burnt-out rubbish and horror by the explosions.

And there were explosions: "I heard at least three, no maybe more…" and, "Yep, it sounded like a war. Why, I recall back in the big war in the south…" and, "The first one was a sound like a shot gun, but those to follow, field cannons for certain and lastly one, big, really big!" The voices on the streets had opinions, ideas, and mostly useless information to add to the sketchy collection of exactly what had occurred. A collection of facts, opinions, and rumors, given to the sheriff from the larger nearby town of Sonora and also to the tiny *Colombia Gazette* newspaper.

This small newspaper slowly hand-set in wood type two whole pages telling its own collected remarks as well as numerous other versions of exactly what happened, how, and perhaps why.

Remains, Assessments, and Reunions

It was a traumatic and painful event for a good many days after, as the sheriff and countless volunteers, including myself, worked to sort out the bodies, miscellaneous body parts, and items of identification, and make an attempt to reunite families with those lost in the explosions.

And there had been four explosions, as witnesses attested to. A small stash of exploded 12 gauge shot gun shell casings was found embedded in the scorched floor planks of the D.O. Miles Bank office, as well as scraps of a couple of leather satchels with traces of black powder embedded, discovered buried beneath the rubble of the back walls of both the bank and water company buildings. It was almost illogical that such a devastating explosion could be the result of a few shotgun shells and a small amount of black powder.

A piece of information later brought to light by a few of the town leaders attested to the existence of a huge underground vault located just behind the bank building, a giant vault dug into the dirt hillside, it was used as a storage facility for all of the black powder in use in the mining community. Its existence was not common knowledge, and regrettably no effort had ever been made to move it away from the growing community of businesses, nor, to reinforce it with iron to make it a safer location for innocent customers inside the businesses as well as anyone sleeping in the rented quarters located directly above them.

Included in the dawn's findings were men and women and six children, remains of two men; one without a leg and one without an eye. These injuries were sustained prior to the explosion and fire.

These disfigurements as well as what few characteristics existed on the bodies, branded them as possible brothers by the names of Hal and Homer Calvin, convicted killers, recently released from the Sonora Jail. In addition, searchers discovered remains of a dark man wearing a gold medallion believed stolen from a stage robbery in the area of Sonora. Despite his injuries, his long hair with pig-tails and facial characteristics marked him as Oriental, a possible match for the outlaw by the name of Po Lim, wanted for crimes all over the gold country from Donner Pass to Fuller's Crossing, Sonora Pass, Jamestown and clear into Mexico.

Subsequent to an intense search of bodies, wreckage, and ashes, was the very apparent absence of Miles Bank manager and Miles Water Company Chairman, D.O. Miles. Likewise, his remains were not among any of the carnage of the dead and dismembered bodies. Miles had disappeared from Colombia, and concurrently, the contents of the two safes under his care turned up missing, contents eventually appraised by a certified bank audit to be in excess of several thousand dollars!

And then, after fallen roof timbers were lifted, and collapsed walls were moved aside, yet another body was discovered within the burnt out ruins of the D.O. Miles Banking establishment. Early identification suggested the body was that of Miles, discovered at last. However, later examination confirmed it could not possibly be that of D.O. Miles, quite impossible; the body was that of...a female!

Past, present, and future.

"Charlotte, however did you talk your sister into coming to that God-forsaken hole of Columbia?" D.O. was forever in her debt, but also uncertain of some of her motives.

"Easy," Charlotte settled back into the cushioned settee, a comfort they shared in their eighth-floor San Francisco hotel room, and continued. "When I told her we would split the money and all she needed to do was sneak into the darkened bank office and knock you out as you tried to abscond with all the funds."

She squirmed in the arms of the chubby man who had removed the funds from both safes prior to their escape. "Shall we have some more bubbly, my cutie?"

"Gentleman." D.O. Miles hefted the chilled quart bottle of what passed for "high quality beverage" from the Pacific Street hotel in San Francisco's Barbary Coast area. He grinned, swung the bottle with enough force to shatter it and crush the skull of the worldly 'Charlotte.'

He had detested her since first meeting her at the bank official's gathering in Stockton, detested her and yet saw a use for her banking expertise, as well as her knowledge of playing people against each other.

"There, all done. Now, we dump your self-centered carcass out the window into the darkness of this blasted winter's cold, and I live comfortably for years on my thousands."

Chubby, and out of shape, D.O. fought to lever the tall body over the wood sash while struggling to maintain his slightly drunken balance, and shove her outward into the blackened night. Miles was unable to maintain any degree of balance on the slippery wood windowsill, and as Charlotte's body slipped free of the window, he lost his grip and in a scream-filled flight, he joined silent Charlotte and the two made the twisting journey downward to the unforgiving stones of Pacific Street, eight stories below.

A fog-chilled dawn found a patrol wagon of the San Francisco Police Department responding in the direction of the slums of Pacific Avenue, responding to reports from an early morning milk delivery dray whose drivers had discovered a gruesome display of crushed death on the roadside. A mixture of mangled body parts was reportedly, "Piled like so much log-wood on the sagging board sidewalks."

Little was said, no tears shed, by the somber group of homeless street dwellers who stopped to gaze and move on. Two brothers lingered, although not to grieve or cry, rather to engage in a frantic search through the pockets of the disgusting tangled mess before the police arrived.

"Holy crow. Lookie here." Patty Masterly held up a double fist-full of what appeared to be real United States hundred dollar bills. "Dammed if we aren't just about to become warm and well fed too." He turned to his brother who had also fetched into bulging pockets and discovered more of the same.

The two, pants and coat pockets soon stuffed with bills, marched off into the bleakness of winter's dawn, headed for the better side of San Francisco, to discover how to live, albeit briefly, on their newly acquired riches.

"SORRY, YOU MISSED THE BOAT..."

L udwig and Anna lived with their seven children in Sotern, Schleswig-Holstein, in northern Germany. They lived on the grounds of the Kaiser's palace, that is to say they lived in the groundskeeper's cottage. Ludwig was the groundskeeper for the Kaiser.

With the changes in the government mood and the pains of another world war, the couple, along with their family decided to immigrate to the United States. The process took a long time and involved not only immigration papers and visas but also acquiring a U.S. sponsor. The couple was lucky, and through friends at their church, acquired information that a German family in the U.S. who owned a large company which built truck bodies, had agreed to sponsor them; that is to help them become located and have some input into acquiring work upon arrival into the U.S. The family name was Fruehauf and still today the family-owned company manufactures large truck bodies with operations on both the east and the west coast.

The agreement was that Ludwig and Anna were to travel alone on a small lumber boat to Southampton, England, where they would board a ship and sail to America. Upon arrival in America, they would be met by members of the Fruehauf family, who would help arrange temporary housing and find some work for the immigrating family. When Ludwig and Anna were financially stable they would send for their children to join them. Meanwhile, the family had set up through their church friends that various families would house and feed the children, and Anna and Ludwig would send money as they earned it; money to sustain the seven children.

The long journey, the cold weather and failing health landed Ludwig in an English hospital the day prior to sailing. He worsened overnight and on the morning the couple was booked to sail to America, the morning of freedom which they had so looked forward to; on a morning of so much hope and optimism…Ludwig died.

That afternoon, April 8, [th] their ship sailed without them, sailed for America, sailed without Ludwig and Anna. Their ship, the R.M.S. Titanic, sailed into history. Because of their financial status Anna and Ludwig would have sailed steerage class on the Titanic. The overall survival rate for steerage passengers; men, women and children, was below twelve percent by some ratings and only as high as twenty percent by others. This terrible death rate was partly due to the fact that gates allowing steerage-class passengers access to the boat decks and lifeboats were locked for some time during the disaster.

It would be weeks before Anna would be aware of what fate had dealt her, with the crushing death of her husband, and the immediate loss of passage to America.

Anna was lost. She spoke almost no English, had just enough money to make ends meet during a two day wait for their sailing date, and was on the street and at a loss as to what to do about her dead husband.

While waiting in the cold lobby of an impersonal British railroad station, she overheard a lady who was speaking German, say her church needed a nannie and seamstress to help make clothing for children without proper garments to go to school. Meekly Anna introduced herself and stated her plight. Almost instantly, as things often work, she was taken in, given a room, a sewing machine and lines of children to sew for. She rummaged through fabric, measured the children, and made them clothing.

She stayed with the Chancellor and Lady Ichord family for six weeks, earned her own room and board, completed far more than the clothing items which the church members had expected, and through earnings and contributions from generous people, saved up money to send home for her children's use, to eventually travel to America.

At last, over three months after her original plans to sail to America, Anna boarded the Olympic, sister ship to the Titanic, and sailed for the new world, sailed for the long delayed entry into American life and a hoped for future reunited with her family.

Upon arrival in the New York Ellis Island Receiving Station, Anna was again lost in an immense crowd, as she was processed along with the typical daily arrival of immigrants amounting to upwards of 1200 men, women and children.

Eventually she was united with the Fruehauf family and was situated in a small room in a dirty, noisy and crowded tenement building. Her job… she was to be a seamstress in a hot stuffy attic of a large fabric manufacturing building. Long hours, uncomfortable and unsafe conditions aside, she survived for twelve months, during which time she scrimped and saved, and sent money off to her children. In just over a year the seven children she had missed so, were able to sail to their new home, their new country, to America, where they joined her. She had good news for them. Through a friend she had met at her new church, she had acquired work in a small town in the state of Nebraska as a fulltime seamstress for an upscale clothing manufacturer, and they were to move into their first house, a small cottage they could call home at last.

Anna and her seven children took a train to Blair, Nebraska, and once again became a united family with clothing, food, shelter and work. The children went to school and to church, acquired small part-time jobs and helped with the costs of living for a family of eight with only one full-time provider.

One of the older sons was hired by the railroad as a telegraph operator and after two promotions was offered a job in San Francisco, California. With careful consideration and prayer, (and some tears too), Arthur set off by train to accept a job as a railroad telegrapher in San Francisco. Within a year the family realized that they wanted to be together, and after selling everything they owned, purchased tickets on the train and in 17 days arrived, not in San Francisco, but due to a mistake in reading tickets, ended up in…Modesto, California.

The family waited in a small Santa Fe station in unfamiliar Modesto while Arthur caught a train from San Francisco to join them. As they waited in the empty train station, in the small town with mostly dirt streets, Anna met a lady with her same first name, who spoke German and was of their church belief. She took them to the basement of her church where they were fed and sheltered until Arthur arrived on a slow freight train. Typical of some men of that time, he caught a ride in the caboose of a valley freight out of Livermore bound, via every small town on the route to Modesto.

When he joined them, he surprised the family with the news that the whole time he had been living in San Francisco he had been studying insurance sales at a small bay area college. Shortley after that, he challenged and passed the insurance agents registry exam, and opened an insurance office in Modesto.

The family soon purchased a large home in central Modesto.

Family members took up various jobs and eventually Arthur announced that he had met a young lady: a young lady who had been invited to the house for a dinner date with his brother, but who instantly fell for Arthur instead and soon, they were married.

All of this took place in the years leading up to 1934 at which point Arthur and his wife Eleanor purchased land in Modesto; two lots, located near the street which became known as Mc Henry Ave. They built a home. Eleanor graduated from San Francisco State University with a master's degree in Education and foreign language. Arthur and his brother-in-law established an insurance agency which, under a different name, remains in business today.

The couple, Arthur Haack, son of Ludwig and Anna Fricke Haack and Eleanor Mary Brophy Haack raised four children, one of whom is Michael Haack, author of this story.

Author's note: While the majority of this writing is true, portions of it are fabricated to add depth and to enhance the reader's enjoyment.

OUT OF THE CANYON

On Monday December 27, with Christmas still fresh in our memories, we left home for a snowshoe packing trip into the Donner Pass Wilderness Area. We had packed into this area for the past two years and each year it got better, as we explored deeper into that peaceful land of scenic beauty off the summit of Highway 50.

However, this year was to be different; vastly different.

Midday we arrived at the summit of Donner Pass and crept through incredible snow depth to the site we had selected for this year's adventures. We were aware of a large season's snowfall but not snowbanks greater than eight feet deep. There was no place to leave a car, and short of climbing a ladder, no way to reach the tops of the snowplow machine built snow packs to search for the trailheads located off the Donner Pass summit.

After two hours dealing with mobs of flatlanders in their stuck cars and dozens of little kids playing in the snow-packed roads, (when you live in a city you always play in the roads, it would appear) we gave up, returned home to plan out an alternate hike and adventure.

We kept everything packed in the car, including equipment for snow camping and four days of eating supplies. We had snowshoes for the hike and crampons and ice tools as we planned to encounter ice conditions.

We typically carried both 12 point crampons and mini spikes called Kahtoola's. In addition to a high-pressure compact MSR stove called a Reactor; we carried an assortment of freeze-dried foods: eggs, lasagna and pasta. We always carried hard candy, bread and jam, oatmeal, dried fruit, chocolate, tea and powder to make hot chocolate.

We had enough experience to know that duck or goose down and wool was necessary to withstand the elements. We had an excellent four-season two-man tent and inflatable micro pads for insulation under sleeping bags (More for an insulator against extreme winter temperatures than for comfort.) We carried emergency bivouac sacks, down coats, snow pants, and numerous layered garments to ensure warmth.

We had a small portable shovel, lights and knives, a camera, GPS, and a state of the arts PLB, (Personal Locator Beacon) used to alert the Air Force national dispatch station in Colorado Springs, who, based on GPS latitude and longitude position fixing, could contact the closest search and rescue organizations. The device was also programmed to contact three selected friends or relatives. We stashed this $500 device deep within a pack with the idea that it was a safety feature we would never use. It carried a hefty fine of $10,000 if used in other than a life-threatening situation.

\<Headed out, at last\>

The following morning we headed up into the Sierra Nevada Mountains toward Ofhausen Ski Resort and a trek down into our revised destination named Water House Canyon.

Herman and I arrived at the turn-off behind Ofhausen Ski area. We slid Herman's Ford Escape into a slight bit of deep snow just off the road and called it good. The trailhead sign read 'Rock and Roll Trail,' perhaps for its undulating behavior as it crawled up the mountain. Overhead looked threateningly like more snow and the predictions were for a major storm, but not right away. The storm was due in four days. Perhaps it had arrived early. With a passing regard for caution based on the weather forecast, we proceeded anyway.

In about ten minutes we were ready with hiking clothing and boots on, snow- shoes lashed to anxious feet, hefty packs tightened on our backs and trekking poles gripped in hands warmed with winter gloves.

We pulled on warm hats and headed up a trail lushly buried in fresh powder upwards of two feet deep.

It was at that point we discovered we had failed to bring the GPS. Turning back seemed unnecessary as I had hiked this area more than once. I failed to mention that two of those times I was alone, and became disoriented following a night or two of heavy snowfall. Both times I had carried a GPS or I might have become lost back then. The other times I had hiked this area with groups. We were more experienced now and there were two of us. The stage was set for one of those adventures later retold from a 'if only we had' standpoint.

Herman was my climbing and packing partner. At seventeen, not just strong, but courageous, he was willing to go all out in sports and adventures.

We ambitiously started up the slightly used trail in deep snow with heavy packs. Herman led and did well, and only eventually slowed a bit, but remained faithful to the job of reiterating the slightly used trail through deep snow while watching for trail markers high up on some trees. Later, we would switch places, so both could feel the challenge of leading and "breaking trail" in deepening snow, while the other partner would enjoy the reward of falling back and relaxing a bit. It was tough going and a long and steep trail lay ahead.

The views along the way included south- facing canyons, *Christmas card* settings of snow draped trees, massive slopes and a "more snow to come" promising sky. Each view demanded camera stops, but today we failed to take time as we were trying to beat the dark which came early at 4:40. At one point we stopped to eat something cold. We sat on our packs and let them carry our weight for a while. We held off setting up the stove but enjoyed the scenery, light talk and a few laughs. After water, fruit, granola bars, and chocolate, we were on our way again.

It had begun to snow harder and we attempted to hurry, but the incline, deep powder and the cold united in a slow approach to the summit.

Water House Canyon, our destination, is not a mile deep or eighteen miles wide such as is Arizona's famous *Grand Canyon*. At best it's just over a mile across and half a mile deep. It has a steep slope from east to west eventually ending at the site of the Norrington Lake resort.

Canyon walls reach about 60 degrees near the top where we had begun our descent.

We set off downhill in a rapidly increasing snowfall. The storm eventually dropped a monstrous four feet in the area.

<Into the canyon>

Herman glanced back, grinned, and stepped off the cornice top, heading downhill in a snowshoeing slide more like skiing in deep powder. I followed a few steps behind, cautious to step into his deep snowshoe tracks, thus avoiding bombarding him with any tiny avalanches I might launch. We had to steer clear of the extremely steep direct descent but rather chose cautious traverses across the canyon as it dropped before us and vanished into the white curtain of falling snow.

This stage of our plan included dropping approximately half a mile to the slightly level area which marked the river ravine itself, then set up the tent and have a base camp. From there we could hike, free of much of our weight, into distant and unexplored areas of the canyon including a frozen waterfall.

Summer circumstances in this canyon were free of the bleakness of snow and ice but incorporated the possibility of bears and the certainty of rattle snakes.

We had selected to deal with the elements of weather rather than unpredictably temperamental creatures.

Anyone who has watched the dreadfully realistic movie 'The Edge,' grasps the concept of the two elements, and while our area lodged the more passive Black bears, rather than the horrible Kodiak Bears, we were not interested in any encounter. We held in high respect California Brown bears and the Western Diamond-Backs from summertime experiences, had plenty of winter snow hiking experiences, and still failed to respect how totally out of control these winter elements could grow to be.

We were anxious to see the site of the Water House pumping station, or what was left of it. The 'Water House,' we were told, was long abandoned and over countless seasons of snow and ice, rain and sun, had gently decomposed.

We anticipated finding only faint markings of the valve and penstock site of a long forgotten water company's failed efforts at controlling snow runoff for that section of the mountains. The plan, to feed captured snow runoff into a small river which was then metered (for a fee) to wealthy summer residents at the high-altitude resort named Pinecrest had failed.

We worked our way across the steep-sided canyon, making traverse after traverse and often changing leads. Ahead and through the escalating snowfall we could faintly distinguish silent trees in soldiered ranks marching toward a destination far below and out of our range of vision. It had become a total whiteout. We could see perhaps fifteen feet ahead, beyond that was unknown territory.

One threat of appalling certainty existed somewhere ahead, existed a vertical drop into an icy channel accommodating the frozen river. While we dared not approach that freezing peril in a state of unprepared blindness, it was included as a day hike with ice tools, crampons, and without the weight of backpacks.

\<Bivouac\>

As it was, conditions shouted the obvious; we were not going to reach that level area today. It was time to consider a bivouac; a temporary site dug into the mountain's steep coating of snow, large enough to house our small tent.

At 3:30 the snowstorm was doing its best to destroy daylight and any thoughts of delaying setting up camp.

Establishing a tent site on a mountainside during a windy snowfall is a thrill, an engineering feat and a juggling act combined, although made vastly easier with two people. First, it's imperative to stomp down the site to form a firm foundation for the tent. Otherwise you will sink in deep with every step and you will sleep in ditches and gullies. We stomped the area, still wearing our packs for added weight and our snowshoes for stronger snow compression. Soon we had a firm and relatively level notch in the mountainside; a significantly secure location for the tent.

The foot-print, a thin nylon layer of insulation is put down first, all the while fighting the snowfall and the whipping wind. Next, the ultra-lite Marmot Alpinist tent, consisting of a fabric body and three slender poles, is snapped together; rapidly a shelter to house two people and their gear. As I drove slender snow spikes into hard packed snow to anchor the four corners and tension lines supporting the tent, Herman was frantically shifting everything from packs into the tent, all the while keeping flying snow outside where it belonged. Snowshoes, poles, crampons and ice tools waited outside the tiny half dome-shaped tent, standing frozen guard against gathering gloom and freezing night. Lastly, our frantically pulled off boots were left in the small vestibule and we dived into the snow free tent, cold but dry!

We had arrived at our home on the cliff side. Outside, the storm increased in fury while indoors we inflated insulation pads, spread sleeping bags and took an inventory of the supplies necessary to survive a major storm for a day or a week.

All this is done in an all-weather ultralight tent about 4.5 by 6.5 feet and 3.5 feet tall.

<Storm>

In the tent we read, talked, played a couple of portable games and fixed food. Preparing a hot meal consisted of locating stove, fuel cell, and igniter and cooking pot. With the Reactor stove these components are all housed in the cooking pot, hence time spent in the search is reduced. Snow is scooped into the pot, and except for nights such as this one, the stove is set up outside and ignited. That night we did the unthinkable and cooked indoors with the door flap slightly open for ventilation; used indoors the stove will kill you with the fumes, or if you're more unfortunate the stove will fall over, ignite your tent and leave you homeless and freezing in seconds. Do not cook in a tent!

We boiled water and added it to freeze-dried meals in pouches and soon enjoyed lasagna and crackers, tea and honey, and hard chocolate. Clean up amounted to putting empty food pouches in our garbage bag, cleaning spoons and closing up the cooled stove.

Disasters typically do not result from a single mistake or error! Disasters they are the sum total of numerous mistakes or incidents which chain together to result in the unexpected. This was the situation that earlier that day, that night, and the following day as one thing after another grouped together, some fate, some error, some most likely the result of poor planning and haste, anyway, each element led to the disaster to follow.

Perhaps the first in a chain of mistakes, was to continue on the hike when a *possible* snow storm was predicted four days off. It came early.

Second was to continue when we realized that we did not have the GPS. Even with the extra confidence of experience and awareness of the area that was an error.

The next error was to fail to place the stove fuel cell in a wool sock and bury it in the foot sack of one of the sleeping bags. This would prevent it, even alcohol based fuel, from freezing.

Now came another bad judgement which could have been no big deal if the fuel cell had not frozen solid. I had failed to place them and the water bottles also deep into sleeping bags.

During that night's long hours, we were occupied slapping the sloped roof and sides of the tent repeatedly. This was necessary in order to eliminate the constant snow build up and allow it to slide down the sides and join the inches of frosty white surrounding our tiny apricot-colored home. During normal sno fall this had never been a problem, however this snowfall was not normal.

We wore our headlamps to bed, but greedily metered their battery power against the darkness. We had two lamps each and extra batteries, but these high power lights gulped batteries like popcorn at a movie, constantly reminding us that when the batteries were dead we faced the dark. We were not, at the time, remotely aware of the demands facing those faithful lamps. It was totally dark by 4:30, and we used one lamp on low setting most of the time until we went to sleep hours later.

Living in a very small tent requires a total conservation of energy and space, as there must be a place for everything or you will move about in the dark and never locate that item you need. Water bottles are stashed alongside the sleeping bags (except during extreme cold when they are placed inside a wool sock and stashed deep in the foot sack of your sleeping bag, along with the fuel cell for the stove.)Most damp clothing is also stashed in the foot sack along with gloves, hats and socks. Food is stored (winter only) in food sacks in the packs at the head of the tent. Headlights, cameras, GPS and PLB are usually stored in the hanging compartments in the top of the tent, high up, near vents, away from moisture.

Sometimes we have slept with lights on heads in the event of something catastrophic on the horizon. It's not fun to grope in the dark for the light you need to locate what you are looking for. Even with this, or any system, often it takes forever to find a spoon at meal time, or to locate the igniter when it's time to start the stove. It's a game really, and laughter, rather than frustration, is the rule when searching for lost items in the tent.

<Night time>

That night it snowed hard and snowed constantly.

I stayed awake a lot so I could worry. That's something I do with immense abandon and a total focused attention. After all, we were well within the range of an avalanche, total burial, suffocation, and just plain becoming lost in the depths of the canyon far below. (I point out that on this trip as on any we had left information with three people as to where we would be, when to expect our return and a phone call to confirm it.) I stayed awake to watch the outside reading thermometer as it crept down toward nineteen degrees. I stayed awake to hammer on the tent roof and sides and dismiss the fallen snow to a ritualistic burial on the ever increasing piles at the base of the tent. I did notice snow build up creeping up the sides of the tent, noticed the icy chill of the tent walls and the weight of snow forcing the tent sides to cave slightly in. I was certain these snow mounds would fall away eventually, they always had before. The chance of burial just did not exist.

Herman often woke to help with the battering of roof and walls and laugh at my concern. "It's night. Go to sleep and worry in the morning; by then there'll be more snow and something worth worrying about."

Now that really helped; but eventually I fell asleep, waking only to force snow off the tent.

Around 0300 something strange happened. The noise of snow falling on the tent ended abruptly and it was very silent. Everyone said yeah the snowfall has ended, everyone being me and with that assurance I fell asleep. Herman slept through it all.

I slept till some faint light entered the tent at about 6:00 am, at which point I unzipped the top of the door and the top of the vestibule. The sight sent me back into the tent, back away from…the edge! Yes, the edge.

In the night the snow had piled up on our bivouac site, built up and totally buried the tent! At some point near morning the tent, and the mountainside became one in a massive slope from its top, above us at the cornice, to the bottom someplace far below among snow and ice and the frozen gorge called Water House Canyon. It was at that point that the sound of falling snow had ended. It still fell, just not directly on the tent!

"Herman wake up!" Nothing. "Herman wake up now, something terrible has happened!" I tried drama but realized I needed to sound authentic too.

"Mmmm, what, what time is it? Ah, boy it's cold!"

"Herman, its nineteen degrees and the tent is buried beneath a massive snow pack and we're on the edge of a cliff leading to the canyon. We got to do something!"

He woke up.

We reopened the top of the tent door and looked out. Snow above, on both sides, and below as far as we could see. It was necessary to scoop away snow in order to further unzip the door and vestibule. Using one of our flat plastic plates we took turns scooping away the snow. It took a while. Hands froze, and breaths became ice, then melted and flowed down inside the tent. Eventually we had enough of an opening in the snow that we could unzip more of the door from the top to within a few inches of the frozen bottom. We very carefully opened the vestibule and I moved partly out, turned to look up and wished I hadn't.

"Oh no!" Oh yes, and I began to shake from the cold and anticipation of the future, and I realized that I was scared.

"Herman, we're part of a continuous slope from the cornice top right down to…well it's out of sight, but I suspect to the canyon floor. There's no flat area anymore."

Acknowledgement of the situation called for some degree of calm, hot food, and a plan.

We talked things over as we prepared to leave the sight.

Any thoughts of firing up the stove, boiling water and warming our bodies with packaged scrambled eggs and hot drinks just did not exist.

In the night all fuel cells and water bottles had frozen solid. We had placed them inside the tent but failed to wrap them in wool socks and place them deep in the foot sacks of the down sleeping bags. Just one more error, or oversight, but in this case one which would haunt us all day as we had very little else to eat save granola bars and frozen chocolate bars.

We discussed the alternatives staying, or leaving, and realized that removing the tent and ourselves from the canyon, while a horrible task even on a normal morning, and was the only choice. The chance of an avalanche, or slipping and falling down that steep snow face was a terrible threat.

We had to dig out the tent, remember it is snowing heavily, almost a whiteout, and find all of our poles, snowshoes, and crampons which were buried in the snow; all buried exactly where we had left them last night in our haste to escape into the tent. We never suspected there would be between three and four *feet* of snowfall during that long and cold night. Later, as we searched the areas surrounding the tent, we discovered that everything was buried except for the handles of the trekking poles protruding scant inches above the deep white, while thankfully helping us locate the remainder of the missing equipment.

Typically, when breaking camp we always took time to carefully organize everything back in the packs. Not so that morning. Today as I sit and write this I am still unable to comprehend how we did it. Herman hurriedly stuffed things into packs inside the tent, while outside I mumbled freezing and unprintable word, and searched for hidden tent stakes frozen hard beneath deep snow. Tent stakes, which were small spiraled aluminum screws, valuable and too expensive to lose, were attached to the tent tabs, and buried beneath the frozen snow.

With freezing hands, which would only function for the task without gloves, I probed and dug and grunted to locate all eight stakes. They had to be removed or the tent would not become free of the icebound mountain face.

Next, we pulled packs from their comfortable rest within the tent, then collapsed and secured the tent to my pack. The tent was our life; it must be treated with full respect. Following that we strapped snowshoes to waiting boots, shrugged into packs, and pulled straps tight.

It was almost time to begin the shockingly unpredictable climb back out. Snowfall being what it was, further time in the treacherous canyon was considered far too dangerous. We had discussed alternatives and decided to climb out, make the return trek to the car, and relocate to a less perilous area.

Prior to leaving, we had prayer. God was always with us and we refused to consider the hike back without His protection. Then we played a quick two out of three rock, paper and scissors to determine who would lead. Herman lost the game, so he led to begin with.

Without hesitation, he addressed the snow wall and set off leading our escape from the canyon. It was 9:15 am, very cold and snowing hard.

<Escape>

Herman lay down a guarded pace up the hill, perhaps because it was extremely steep, perhaps because it was very deep snow, maybe due to the slightly diminished visibility, and certainly because there was one speed up out of that canyon; very carefully slow. I followed in his steps, which did not amount to much as with each step almost all the snow fell back into the previous tracks and you started again, digging with the toe of the snowshoe and then stamping down until there was a deep, firm footing forced into the wall. Like climbing ice except ice usually will support you rigidly. This stuff just fell apart, crumbled, balled, sank deeper, and then rolled downhill.

All too soon it was my turn, and while I was glad to take my share of the lead, I rapidly realized that as I took over that I was fighting a fearsome battle. It was almost impossible to balance. Many times I literally fell forward, to the side, and almost rolled backward. Hard as it was, I refused to fall, as it could prove impossible to regain your footing on such an incline with what weight as we carried, and fighting the unstable deep snow. In a fall I suspected I would end up dead, buried at the bottom of the frozen cliff. I leaned forward; thrust a foot shod in a snowshoe deeper into fluffy powder and managed an anchor.

One step, up and slightly closer to the top, clear the area above, now another, repeat, repeat, repeat. Up and up we went, agonizingly slow. Dig, dig, mash, mash, lean and dig again and step harder and lean further. Then repeat it again, and again, and again. I prayed, prayed hard. I was scared. At one spot I suspect, but for my partner's existence and a slight degree of pride, I would have given up. It was awful, energy sapping, hardly productive, and freezing, freezing, freezing cold. Even with the constant work and energy expended, I never felt a single degree of warmth; just cold and cold and cold. And we climbed on. Turn and turn about we just kept making slow progress, and yet, as I took my turn leading, I felt as if energy were slipping away like water down a drain.

At various points we changed positions on the wall again and again.

Eventually Herman disappeared ahead of me in a courageous mustering of extreme youthful power. He was waiting for me at the top. "So, what took you so long?"

A big grin. Smart Alec.

"I had to wait for a freight train at the crossing!" I was ashamed of my slow progress. "What the heck you think held me up? It's steep!" I was feeling beat, worried, cold and frightened too. Besides all of that, I was already very hungry and realized that anything hot was just not going to happen. "Hell that was horrid. I'm bashed." I uttered my feelings in a scream.

He looked way too calm and relaxed. Oh well, seventeen years old gives you a lot that my unmentionable age takes away. A teacher friend at school where I teach always referred to me as *the man with driver's license Number One*. The kids love it. Friends!

We took time to say our thanks to God who had made it possible to escape that canyon. A canyon which, as we looked back down into its deep cavernous maw, gave precious little indication of what rested far below in the invisible snow filled reaches. I moved further away then realizing that I had experienced far too much and even standing near the cornice frightened me.

As you read this and examine our gross errors and make your own judgement calls, remember, we were not careless overall. We did not just go off and try to die doing something stupid. We did not fail in our escape plan, we were just totally unable to judge the power of the storm nor the monumental effect it had on any system of safety and escape we had in our bag.

We had reached the top of the cornice in almost two hours. It had taken us approximately 45 minutes to make the trek down to where we had set up the bivouac.

We looked upward and ahead at the snow fall. It was coming down really hard, and realizing that we did not have the GPS with us, looked for our tracks from having hiked in only 24 hours ago. Stupid vain effort, of course with the almost three feet of fresh snowfall we found none at all.

I glanced at a watch and decided it was already too late to stop for food, although it would be just a handful of something cold.

We started off on what was feasibly supposed to be two hours trekking downhill to the patiently waiting warm shelter of the heater-equipped car.

When you snowshoe with a heavy pack it's easy to fall if you lose any degree of balance, unless you are quick and regain stability. I did a lot of that in the next six or so hours, over and over again. Most likely, that did no good for my back problem. Herman fared better, with maybe one slight stumble and one fall.

We had what seemed like miles of uphill and slight downhills to cover, whereas, on the way in it had been all uphill. We kept on stepping ahead, one step, another, another, and another. Each step required planting the snowshoe, forcing it to mash down the snow so you didn't lose balance and fall as it settled further. Then when it was all settled, you shifted your weight onto the forward leg and did the same thing over again, and again, and again, carefully, very carefully. Now when it's time to lift the back foot and move it forward all you have to do is lift five or so pounds of snow that had settled onto the snowshoe when it's deep in the hole,. Lift it all up, dump it, shift forward without falling, and repeat it, and repeat it, and repeat it.

On a good day, with less soft snow and slightly less weight perhaps this is fun. You talk and look at scenery, take photos, stop for snacks and meals, and progress along. Not so today. It is so very cold, the way so hard, and my old back injury was making itself well known. All things considered, it was only ugly, tediously hard work. And now, after refusing to face it for over two hours we had to face a new terror slowly creeping up on the horizon. Without the GPS and no old tracks to follow, we were lost!

\<Lost\>

"George, you've hiked this trail more than I have." Desperation now? "Don't you recognize anything?" Herman was hoping I could distinguish from thousands of gathered pines, all heavy laden with snow, all facing different directions and all merging in fictitious pathways leading to... to nowhere.

"No, I don't know for sure. It all looks exactly the same. I've been in this area with a group or a GPS, but to distinguish a trail now, I can't." Now what?

Herman seemed unconcerned at the time, "Well we're close to the trailhead. I know that, so, we just go on. I suspect perhaps between those two trees over there."

He would gesture in the direction of some tall evergreens, as though they were the unusual trees guarding the gateway to freedom and escape, rather than the gateway to further trekking in a random and questionable direction.

Isn't that the basic definition of getting lost; wandering aimlessly? We did that, and did it for upwards of six-plus hours. We did it as the weather deteriorated, as we grew hungry and thirsty. We did it as we failed to focus on anything other than obtaining the trailhead and a warm car. We did it so intently that we passed up an essential building block of survival: energy! We robbed the energy needed to fill the stomach that it might feed the blood, and give sugar to the hungry brain, and feed the endlessly overworked and starving legs.

There was an additional haunting fear in my mind, "We dare not wander off the mountain and go back deep into that horrid canyon; we just can't!" Therefore, subconsciously I suspect, I never allowed us to journey much to the right or north direction, which, in my estimation would deliver us back into the clutches of Waterhouse Canyon.

Enter yet another of the chain of factors leading to disaster: energy starved muscles and blood-starved brains: two elements of hypothermia. Next would come dementia, disorientation and sleep.

Again, as you read this, as you perhaps vicariously participate in the nightmare, you will say such things as, "Well why didn't they do this, or that was so stupid, they should have done this."

Starved brains, freezing bodies, empty stomach, and the onset of hypothermia are words on the page, you don't get to enjoy them as a reader. Sorry.

Eventually the old climbing spinal damage grew worse and became a back throbbing nightmare. It grew increasingly as the day proceeded, typical for this lower back injury of about 30 years. I stopped at last.

"Herman, I can't take it. Maybe I am a weakling!" Almost a plea, but slightly angry too. "I'm just going to pieces and can't make it further!"

He turned back and faced me. He looked at me with understanding and friendship on his face. "You're my friend and I would never call you weak. You have an injury and need to get some relief." His comment showed an understanding flowing with a balm of comfort.

"I'm sure that our trail head is nearby. We'll reach the car soon now." I worked the words to reassure myself as well as Herman.

And then, as we moved ahead into more cold, falling snow, and lost directions, I made a further stupid decision of the evening.

In a state of hypothermia when the mind moves into areas not normally entered, I decided...I *think I'll leave my pack under this tree at the trail's edge.*

I unstrapped the 55 pound pack, slung it off into the snow and continued to move ahead. As Herman was leading at the time, he did not see me make this terribly stupid move. This very act, in time, would prove to be a serious error in judgement. Just another rick in the wall leading to disaster.

The pack settled quietly into the snow, and I moved ahead. *Aaaah, less pain, more comfort.* I still carried the feeling attached to any form of giving up. The word baby came to mind, but I focused on the job at hand, Survival.

I encouraged myself, *I'm sure that our trailhead is nearby. We'll reach the car, leave all the gear and I can return on a well-stomped-down trail, grab my pack, trek out to the car and be on our way.*

It sounded very simple as we continued to wander, cold and lost, but me, without the pack. A pack which contained my life sustaining down-sleeping bag our tent, and our lifesaving Personal Locator Beacon, our PLB.

Later on, I broke trail with no pack to hinder me and Herman never realized I was without it. We moved ahead, still in deep snow, with more falling, and still lost, but now we headed, into full darkness.

"George, I've about had it." Perhaps two hours later. "Ahead, see those thick power cables overhead?" Herman pointed up and ahead about a hundred yards. "I don't recall them on the way in. We're still lost and need to turn back."

I wanted to go on. Somehow going on meant sooner or later we would be at the car. Little did we know it but at the point where we turned around we were about 800 yards from the car, just under the power lines and around a steep right hand turn. Had we continued would we have missed the shinning object of relief and escape, missed that fortress of safety, missed the car, as the car was totally buried beneath the deep snow? So, we turned back.

One hour of further trekking back on our trail where some indication of our snowshoe tracks still slightly recognized beneath the still falling snow. The snowfall had decreased somewhat.

Then Herman announced something that scared me.

"George I can't stand this cold any longer. I'm freezing and my toes ache terribly." He looked slightly haggard and I realized for once he was in pain. "I just want to stop and get into a sleeping bag right now!"

I recognized a startling fact. In the three years or more of hiking and packing with Herman, he had never complained; he just doesn't do that.

I recognized symptoms of pain and impact of cold, was worried and agreed at once."Yep let's get you into down and into your emergency bivouac sack.

I pulled out his down sleeping bag, stuffed it into an emergency bivouac bag of super thick aluminum, with a layer of reflective material on the inside. The emergency bevy is not a tent, but against harshest conditions, it is something to include in your pack. It makes a lot of difference. He had on gloves, hat and a fairly convincing smile too.

At that point he asked me, "George, where is your backpack?"

Hell, no, not that. Not a missing backpack. I could not believe it, my pack, resting place of the lifesaving PLB and all my down comforts... my backpack was, gone!I told him I had no idea but guessed I had just removed it in a state of hypothermia, of a total loss of brain power, of absurdity.

It was a testimony to his condition that he did not just jump up and kill me on the spot. He was relatively calm.

"George, you have 'til 10:30 at the latest to return with your pack. After that I'll stuff everything back into my pack and come after you. Do you understand?"

This was a serious young man. "You stay on what remains of our snowshoe trail all the time. Don't leave for anything. Understand?" He looked harsh. I was worried, or scared.

"Don't worry.' I had encouragement in my voice. I would be able to follow our tracks to a fair degree. "The trail will be a highway by then, watch out for high- speed skiers. I'll be back soon." Why not? No worries.

\<Separated\>

We both wore our high power headlights, which when attached to the head put out some serious light. We each had two, one for a backup as a result of a nighttime return, months past, on an icy trail out from Yosemite Falls.

I moved on snowshoes along an upward bound trail, slightly trekked down now, moved off a ways turned back once to wave and be assured he would be ok. He grinned, waved, and then the steep hill and falling snow hid him.

I trekked a ways, stopped, and prayed for Herman's safety and that I would find the missing pack too. I turned then, turned away, rubbed my eyes and trekked on up that trail toward my pack, the tent, my down bag and our emergency PLB, a device we had agreed, "We'll always carry it but never need to activate."

The extremely powerful headlight I wore that night blew away darkness, falling snow, and any worry attached to the unknown night. I moved fairly rapidly along scant remains of the trodden trail we had previously laid down. Moved without a pack, and in about an hour and ten minutes I came upon a dark lump on the side of the trail near a small tree. Sure enough, it was my pack resting quietly beneath a thick layer of fresh snow.

I was there and stood a few minutes to say thanks to God, eat some of a dry, frozen granola bar, and try to have a sip from my water bottle, which remained tightly frozen. Even carried close to the body, they would not have thawed in the cold which registered 14 degrees when I found my thermometer attached to my pack later on.

Nothing left to do but stagger about, slipping that heavy pack onto a sore back. It was finally on but the back was unhappy. I was twisted and so were the straps. In a few minutes I had readjusted things, tightened the pack and slipped gloved hands into trekking poles, checked my watch and planned about a forty-five minute return trek to Herman.

I fed on that idea like a starving hiker consumes food and drink. Oh how the powerful darkness must have enjoyed its bit of irony.

\<The fall\>

I started off as you do on snowshoes with a slightly wide stance, and avoiding the opposite shoe as you step. It's a practiced gait and makes a slightly different but required footing. I stepped forward, missed the position and stepped on my own foot and lost balance! With my weighty pack also off balance I shot forward off the trail and rolled several times, a rather clumsy, lopsided flopping roll, jettisoning trekking poles at the end. I fairly flew downward, and abruptly stopped at the bottom of a ravine when I landed on a small frozen river.

Deep in my self-inflicted avalanche, and slightly tangled in snowshoes and gear I frantically struggled to get away realizing that beneath the ice-surface was frozen water ready to burst and swallow me.

I crawled but was unable to stand, unable to walk. My back was on fire with the new injuries, and pain floored me right back onto the ground. I was stranded off the trail and down about thirty feet, out of view perhaps too.

Then Herman's parting words came to my mind: "You stay on that trail all the time. Don't leave it for anything. Understand?"

I understood that I was terrified and injured, and off the trail! Lost off the trail and no one would know for sure where. Quickly, I attempted to struggle uphill, but succeeded only in sliding back to where I had landed.

Now I was scared. I screamed to God, "Have you forgotten me? What do you plan to do - just leave me here?" Funny thing, how fear turns quickly to anger. I was angry and hated myself for it. I tried again. "God, help me, I am really injured and can't go on alone."

He took over.

I lashed out in the darkness, first locating my trekking poles which had somehow followed me downhill, then unbuckled the pack, which I dumped onto the ground beside me. Had I carried a climbing rope this would have been much easier, but the rope was in Herman's pack.

First I removed snowshoes and attached my crampons to my boots. Then, using a carabineer, I clipped the handles of my trekking poles to the top handle of the heavy pack, and attempted to crawl uphill and drag the pack. Nothing worked as the heavy and uneven pack dug itself deeper into the snow. Maybe if I pulled it on the other side which was slightly curved and smoother. I tried the reverse side and sure enough, we advanced a slow inch after sluggish inch, but it was progress.

A million years later... ok perhaps twenty minutes later, I reached the trail again. I was back on track, but realized with a degree of horror that I could not walk! Not just sore now, my back was injured deeply. No standing. No walking, I was stranded! However, I was back on the trail, such as it was.

Panting with exploding breaths, I laid out the pack, poles, my removed crampons, and myself directly on the trail. No one was going to miss me now even if all they found was a frozen solid corpse.

I actually remember sort of chuckling at the morbid thought as I stood back and watched a rescue party rounding the corner, and with aghast expressions, discovered a slightly animated and frozen corpse blocking the trail. I had come a long way from my death fear back down in the steep gully.

Fingers out of gloves shook, buckles refused to respond as I fumbled with the pack zippers, and settled for the tent footprint; thin fabric but once folded over it offered some of the much needed insulation. I slipped my inflatable air pad out of its cover, but my breath refused to supply necessary pressure to inflate it. I took what it offered, along with snow pants, heavy boots and down parka. I rolled up in what I had and tried for logical thinking.

All things considered, injury, being lost, stove failure, separated, starving, dehydrated, and freezing, it was time to make a very difficult decision; one that once made could not be reversed. Also, once made, announced our desperate condition to all, l and if used incorrectly held a hefty $10,000 fine too. As I lay there alone, cold, in horrible pain, and slightly scared too, I realized that I must activate the PLB. Once decided, it seemed the absolute right thing to do and there was no going back.

Deep in my pack rested the very High-Tec device, about 4 by 6 inches and perhaps 3 inches thick. It housed a GPS, transmitter, message screen, and a powerful white flashing strobes; all designed to announce "Help!" It was safety, hope, and a rescue at a hefty, $500 price tag.

<The P.L.B.>

I removed the device from its small case, held it in my lap and asked God for direction. It was quiet, cold, and as I considered my situation I visualized how things must have been for Herman way back there, *alone* on the freezing trail.

No going back now, I removed the antenna from its locked and folded position built into the side of the piece of equipment. In so doing, the well hidden transmit switch, a rather large and deep seated button, and came into plain view. Do or die, I pressed the button down. Nothing. Had it died already? No! Not now! Not when we needed it so greatly. I read the brief instructions and again I pressed the button, this time holding it for the prescribed five seconds. Lights came on, the built-in strobe light flashed a powerful five thousand lumens up into the heavens for any passing aircraft, and the lifesaving information began to move across the built-in screen: latitude, longitude, names of addressed recipients and more.

It was 1830, 6:30 pm. I was both relieved and scared. What if this was not a life and death situation, then what? Again, I sent prayers upward, far beyond what that tiny man-made device reached. My pleas reached a much more powerful rescuer; my message reached God. It reached a God who is there for everyone at all times and was there for Herman and for me that cold and frightening night. He had already gone to work when our tiny machine began sending forth its meager earthly pleas. Both powers worked but in addition faith was needed. I looked around for mine and discovered in desperation I needed more than I seemed to have.

I set the device atop my pack then, certain that the additional inches would assure a successful transmission.

Now it was time to take store of a few things. I looked around and found snowshoes, trekking poles, and crampons and placing them upright in the snow nearby. I wanted to know exactly where they were. My light was still affixed to my head, but I also removed an additional headlamp from a stubbornly zippered side pocket of my pack, along with a small pack of trail mix which I began to chew on. Water or not, I was going to get back some much needed energy. I rechecked my water bottles, but they were both frozen solid. Wool insulation wraps for those precious water bottles were critical to survival.

A long and steep mile away Herman, performed the ritual keep warm activities I had discussed and taught: including: singing, waving arms, jumping about and returning to the down bag. I practiced the same, waved arms, sang songs, waved arms and attempted to stand and dance about for warmth. The legs just failed to extend and so I did my dancing on the ground. It worked, and I kept on doing it as did Herman a cold and solitary mile away.

That night I prayed for him, prayed for my daughter whom I realized was on the contact list from the satellite station in Colorado. She would know only that the emergency transmitter had activated and we were in some danger. She was devastated as well she might be.

Eventually her husband's father, a Modesto doctor who owned a private plane, flew to her home in Napa, returning her to their home outside of Hughson, Calif., so she might have their company and the certain hope that comes from group prayers. Her husband was at work and had to remain in Napa.

Meanwhile, the system had also contacted Herman's mom. She was equally devastated and uncertain. She gathered family for prayers that continued far into a dark night and portions of an uncertain day too.

Two others were contacted through the system: a mountaineering friend from church and his wife. They loaded their car and drove to the trailhead site we had informed them ahead of time which we would hike from.

At the trailhead, they encountered a snowbound car. The only problem, was they looked for my red Jeep Rubicon and found, very deeply buried in the snow, Herman's Ford Escape, which my friends did not even know existed. Wisely prepared for the unknown, they made a phone call to a police officer friend who ran the license plate on the Ford, which came back belonging to Herman's mother.

They were at the right place and parked there all night, as rescue crews arrived, became stuck and broken down in the deep snow, had to abandon rescue until dawn, and the blessed reduction of the seemingly endless snowstorm.

Meanwhile, at my end, all I knew for certain was that the PLB had transmitted the messages. Its information flowed peacefully and continually across the screen including latitude and longitude and numerous pieces of technical data. I knew this was transmitted, but as with any blind transmission there is always an uncertainty...was it received?

I somehow drifted off and awoke at about 2300, 11pm, and realized that I had actually slept and was instantly alerted to the fact that I heard my name called.

"George, George!" This followed by a long and sharp whistle and another and another. The Morse code I had taught Herman chirped out in crisp bursts across the cold night's distance.

How far away was he? How long had he been calling? Was he nearby? Was he about to give up in desperation? Then a bright light flashed across tree tops from a nearby dip in the trail. Herman was close and attempting to reach me.

<Reunited>

I jumped up, realized I could not stand or walk, and fell down and rolled part way back down the steep trail. Flailing arms stopped me as legs with no power flopped about in the icy cold snow. Using arm strength alone I pulled myself upward, once again back to where my equipment waited patiently. Then with a raspy voice I lashed out at the unforgiving night's blackness, "Herman, I'm here!" I think I tried to whistle but frozen lips sent forth a week "pffft" and little else.

Inside a pack pocket I discovered a whistle and a light and made contact if only slightly muffled. It didn't matter, he had heard me and shortly we were rejoined. The first thing he exclaimed was, "Oh, oh my gosh; you activated the PLB!"

I explained the fall, the impossible pain in back and legs which refused to walk and the ultimate decision to call for help. He had already considered it an essential and so we were in agreement.

"How long ago did you activate it?" He asked.

"Er...several hours..."

"But," he was uncertain then, as was I, "where is the rescue?"

While neither of us was even remotely aware of all that was required to initiate a search, we assumed that they would be on the way in about an hour and on site in only a couple more.

We managed to get into sleeping bag atop deflated mattresses, better than nothing but freezing snow. I pulled out my down parka and struggled shivering arms into it.

Warmth flowed over me. We joined in further prayer and continued attempts at keeping warm during the remainder of the very cold and uncertain night.

We discussed all that had occurred during the hours we were apart. No one slept much, the fear of the eternal sleep of the frozen kept us alert, plus we were certain *they* would be there any moment with rescue, although we had no idea just how long this might take. Disappointment and fear reappeared as we recognized how many hours had passed since I had activated the PLB. We had no concept as to what was involved in forming and activating a trained rescue party.

Throughout that long night we continued to sing songs and pray, with the certain knowledge that sleeping in the deep cold was potentially dangerous. We both recognized these facts from study as well as practice in the field. With this knowledge, we should have eliminated the chain of mistakes ending with us in this situation.

As it tends to do, the termination of night brings the blessed relief of dawn. Some arrived as a fiend bearing further bleak and unpleasant storms some approached as a light wind and snow. This dawn floated in bearing a calmer winds, a lighter snowfall, some signs of a possible clearing sky and a nine degree surface temperature. The snow covered all with the cold hard paw of her relentless frost.

We moved about to crack loose the frozen coating which attempted to contain our small surroundings of thin fabric and down bags. Once freed, Herman, nursing icy fingers from damp gloves and ice-bitten toes still deep inside a down bag, decided to attempt again to activate the forever dead and dying cell phones we carried. While we had tried the night before without any service, he continued to attempt of reach the 911 services. There still hung over our unfaithful minds an uncertainty that the PLB had in fact reached help.

<911>

We attempted the phone, and sang out our prayers too. Thirty-first dialed attempts failed then:

"911, what is your emergency?" Herman was connected, and so astonished he failed at once to answer. "911, what is your emergency? You have reached the emergency system for the Stanislaus and Tuolumne County. What is your emergency?"

Now he was ready.

"My name is Herman Ruple. We are lost someplace behind the Ofhausen Ski Resort. I have some frost-bitten toes and my partner has a severe back injury and cannot walk. Please do not hang up as we might not be able to reconnect. The service here is terrible."

"I understand you are lost in the snow country near Ofhausen. What is your partner's name? Is it George Bakker?

What on earth.... "Yes, it is, and he has a back injury and can't walk out. We are lost and I have some frost-bitten toes too. How did you know his name?"

Perfectly logical question.

"We understand. Your PLB sent information to NORAD last night, who also contacted us last night at about 1830. Immediately we activated a search and rescue, with teams sent your way. Unfortunately, the storm was so severe that they could not get through last night, and are waiting for further trained team members this morning, as soon as they regroup they will come to your rescue. Do not worry, help is on the way. Also, your family phone numbers were contacted last night. Do you understand this?"

We were both alert and alive now. "Yes, oh yes. We do understand and will remain on the phone. Please, can you contact our family members and encourage them that we are ok and will be rescued? They must be very worried by now."

He recited the phone numbers for his mom, my daughter, and our friends who often hiked and traveled with us. He stayed on the line for some time. Eventually the voice at 911 told us to stay exactly where we were and be assured the rescue teams, now three in number, were on their way to our latitude and longitude, and could be expected to arrive around ten o'clock. We both expressed our genuine thanks to the operator and the system he represented. The signal ended.

We looked at each other with what could only pass as a combination of astonishment, confused relief, and thankfulness. What to do first? We prayed, although we had been so certain of rescue and yet so uncertain too that it seemed difficult to decide exactly what to say. We joined in what perhaps remains the most powerful of all prayers, The Lord's Prayer.

What followed, may seem to the casual reader to be anticlimactic. It was in fact, the climax to all that went before. About 10:15, in what was an obvious lull if not an end to the snowfall and a degree of filtered sunline, voices came up from the nearby downhill calling out, "Is anyone there?"

We shouted back "Yes, yes, we are here. We are Herman Ruple and George Bakker. We are the ones you are searching for."

No good letting them wander off assuming we were casual campers.

We reiterated our calls at least twice more.

Soon, a trio appeared up the slight hill, three men in red parkas with large packs, traveling on cross country skis and pulling a rescue sled.

\<Rescue\>

"We have visual contact now," one member voiced into his radio. Soon the rest of the party arrived and there was a joint venture of assessment of patients, collection of assorted packing, climbing, and general camping gear, distribution of blessedly steaming drinks of tea and soup, and rubbing of frost bitten toes. "Nope, only stage one. They will be fine soon," to Herman's relief. Then the question, "Can either of you walk out? You are not far from the trail head!"

Not far? But we were lost.

It turned out that when we turned back last night, we were just at the power lines, and around a turn, perhaps 1 mile was...our car! We were there but failed to recognize any signs, and turned back to encounter injury and additional loss.

In time, the rescuers were joined by a lady who also worked rescue with a nearby resort, and had skied down below the power lines in case we were up that way. She arrived with a sled and asked if either of us needed evacuation. Herman was fine, and it seemed that in the morning my legs, with snowshoes and no pack, could walk a well-tramped trail out. With everything lashed to sleds behind the rescuers, with us lashed to snow shoes, and lead by the men in red we were on the trail once again.

A stranger trail than last night. That morning's trail wore the appearance of a well-packed snow path with sides rising upwards of two feet.

We trekked that same snow trail in daylight with a much diminished snowfall, and saw ahead those thick overhead power cables which assured us that we were lost last night, and enacted the misjudged reversal of our trek.

Under the power lines and perhaps a quarter mile farther, we rounded a steep snow-banked curve and perhaps a further quarter mile ahead lay the small parking area including a massive mound of snow which would in time turn into Herman's car. A few worthwhile strides more and we were there. Almost by magic the first people we saw were our two friends from home, standing together, man and wife, with cups of hot coffee, chocolate, and soup in hand.

<Friends>

Friends are like that. Just normal people, who turn into saints, doing the impossible at exactly the right time, without a backward glance or a single thought for the time, effort or cost involved. Thanks were even waved aside as we attempted to show how truly overwhelmed we were with all that had occurred that day.

We spent some valuable time that morning saying thanks to a lot of people who had made a difference in our lives. We took considerable time discussing what had gone wrong, and what to do right next time. We stumbled over words explaining how much it had all meant to us, as help arrived from far off and the consideration given without a cent exchanged in return.

We stood together that morning with our new, as well as old friends, friends who worshiped weekly with us, who stood beside us in good and bad, and joined us then in prayers of thanksgiving for lives spared, for hope renewed. We spoke to a God who is, in our belief, very much a part of each day throughout the years as we make our way through the darkness, as well as the sunshine of life.

Eventually, we called family members and assured them that we were well and on the way home soon. Only then, as we recognized starvation, we all drove to a nearby restaurant, where we ate what was later described as a "considerable meal" to make up for the fact that over the past 24 hours no food, and precious little beverage, had passed either of our throats.

Feebleness flew as energy returned. My back remained in terrible pain almost impossible to focus through and yet some relief came with pain medication and the knowledge that in time it too would be just fine.

\<Home\>

Eventually we left, headed down the hill toward homes and families and soon were in range of cell phone connection too. News of our safety had reached them far sooner, but our voices over the waves gave back all that had been lost over those past troublesome hours. With restored cell phone connection Herman spoke to his mom. I spoke to my daughter. Cheers and tears flowed, and within a couple of hours, sooner perhaps, we were in fact, home.

\<Hospital\>

I managed for two days of terrible pain and gave up. With my doctor's, my daughter's, and my friend's encouragement, I was at the ER, and then into the hospital for a very drugged and fuzzy four days.

They say I had plenty of friends visiting, encouraging me and showing me the love that our God has offered us all, freely offered. I believe it, I just remember very little of it.

My daughter and son-in-law were there most of the time, Herman and his mom were there most of the time, the principal and two teachers from the school where I taught as well as a doctor friend and my own personal doctor visited too.

Our God, our friends and our families are the reason we both survived out there.

\<Recovery>

Herman's toes recovered, but ache when it's cold. He is anxious to be back up on a trail as am I. Since the hospital event I have taken medication, have received three epidural spinal injections, endured physical therapy and ultimately spinal surgery. There is, along with much relief still some lingering pain. "In time," they say. "In time."

I am a very impatient man and "In time," scares me. In time I was again up a wilderness trail with a pack on, across an unmarked snowy meadow in search of nameless beauty to record on camera and in mind, over a steep mountain pass on my bike, and away from the everyday flatlands of home.

God cares a lot. I have hiked, biked, swam, snowshoed, climbed and continued with most normal activities. Running is a difficulty which I have to come to terms with, perhaps no more marathons for me. However, we constantly remind ourselves, we are safely off the mountain and alive to tell the story, as the saying goes.

\<Authors Note>

Although this is a true story in a book of mostly fiction, I have changed names of those involved as location names to keep it from being just another personal account of an everyday event.

WAITING FOR EDITH

In an early November snowstorm of that year, I loaded climbing gear, a compact stove, food and a bivouac into my old Land Rover. The 4WD machine had seen better days, but then so had British Leyland Motors. Its paint and upholstery revealed years of hard usage, but tires, gears and engine held out against the Berkhalden mountain conditions. At 10,300 feet it was not the highest mountain pass, but road conditions and trails taxed good drivers, hikers and climbers, and that weekend I was in line to be all three.

My work, as jobs tend to, had kept me far too late that Friday, so after an uphill 'chug chug' to Berkhalden, I was hiking into the mountainside hanging meadow of choice with a headlamp, and pushing aside determined sage, juniper brush and snowshoe-deep powder. Setting up my camp consisted of dropping my pack, rigging a bivouac sack, throwing myself and my gear inside and sleeping.

I did open a Dewar bottle and drank down the contents: a stomach warming concoction my brothers and I, in years past, had named "Cycler's Tea." It was comprised of things which invoke images of a joint venture of Devonshire High Tea and a bad night in a climber's camp. Mainly it was orange tea, honey, a generous shot of Ficklin Port, a trace of Peppermint Schnapps and a large drop of lemon oil for tang. Once downed it was wise to be near a resting place because very shortly, you're done.

I awoke at dawn.

As things tend to be on the Berkhalden, weather conditions made a considerable change in the night. I woke to vastly more snow, and while not enough to dampen my spirits, conditions required continued use of snowshoes for any progress forward into the high country.

Within an hour, I had stuffed hot oatmeal, raisins and honey inside my stomach and drenched it with a blend of foo-foo, chocolate and vanilla. Soon after that, I had packed climbing gear, rope, and chocolate bars into a pack and headed out on a slippery uphill slog.

Eventually, the climb to my favorite rappelling ledge demanded a bit of boots fitted with Kahtoola crampons against the slippery surface.

Without a partner I was reluctant to join forces with what would have been the more typical two-man ventures, so I stuck to a known overhanging ledge or two, and a further trek uphill to the 11,500 foot Ausladen Peak, the best overlook on the ridge.

The rest of the weekend was quiet winter's solitude in the heavenly elevations which included a couple of further treks to some icy cracks and various points of spectacular views down into valleys of central Bavaria, only ending in the usual, *You've got to go back to work* outlook.

Parts of me remained atop the peaks, but the rest, including gear stowed in a pack and snowshoes firmly lashed to reluctant boots, headed back downhill to my partially-buried old green contraption. Halfheartedly, the truck and I faced the journey downhill by three o'clock, intent on arriving in the proximity of Aeyerdang Air Force Base, by six pm. That allowed for a stop at a slight notch in the mountain named Mitthausen, where a longstanding hostel I had heard about named Ruheplatz supplied hot food and dark ale; the cure to fend off hunger and sleep, until I landed in my home quarters.

The downhill trip was slow and more or less relaxed, save for the rumble of treaded tires against rough ice-capped ruts, and the strangely comforting smell of oil, rubber and engine heat.

I spiritually revisited the weekend and considered where I would go next time. The same mountain held enough intrigue to call me back weekends for eternity, thus I stamped it into my mental calendar and said, "Yeah, can't wait" out loud, and took the next curve slightly too fast.

Ok, time to focus…more or less.

The old machine had a typically British motorcar-inadequate heater; hence I was ready for the hostel at Mitthausen and any warmth it offered.

Hostel Ruheplatz, when I arrived, was something I was not prepared for: a physical warmth and a spiritual atmosphere plying comfort unexpected in the rough high country.

Once inside, and seated at a small table fireside, I relaxed and took time to inspect the surroundings. The hostel was old wood and stone construction and in some past years had served a fairly large tourist crowd.

Beyond the warmth extended by logs ablaze in a great stone fireplace, a plank and beam timber construction with rough wood furniture, was the cordiality extended by the greeter who introduced herself as Edith. Aged with wrinkles and a weathered smile, she took my order, delivered delicious hot food from a back room kitchen and in time shared conversation with a sincerity missing in the flash and flurry associated with typically disinterested workers at take-out bistros.

I had introduced myself as Eric, looking the tall and slightly tired traveler with blond hair and blue eyes. Meanwhile Edith joined me in relaxed conversation by the fire where she enjoyed a glass of burgundy and me, a second dark Hack Beck.

She gave me some history of the hostel and surrounding area too. "This place was built before 1880. That's when the railroad ran right behind the building and brought freight, hungry passengers and a steady flow of mountaineers to rent the rooms upstairs." She stopped and looked slightly saddened by memories of those days; days well before her time.

She continued, slower now, "The war, the changes of the main railroad freight and passenger routes, and a close-by, all-weather road took their toll. We get fewer guests, although thankfully enough to stay in business year round."

"And for that I am grateful." I only then realized my fortune for the food, the warmth; certainly the hospitality and conversation.

I prolonged the conversation with interest. "Have you worked here for long? While this place appears to be rather remote, it seems to be surviving even in the snow season." I suddenly felt like I had trespassed into what might be a private quarter and wished that I had not spoken.

Edith was far too mature for such worry, "Oh, I have plenty to keep occupied. I have part time work at the railroad freight station. The Trans Europe Express may not pass here but there is a daily AlpenZug bringing freight, mail and the odd passenger."

Her smile brought back some of the lost warmth to the conversation. "Often they will bring a whole family who might stay over all weekend at the hostel, giving me further work getting them settled in and fed." She smiled with the comforting thought that she was not yet redundant; unnecessary. With something like guarded hesitance she glanced about the room, pausing to discover the slumbering man across the room by the fireside, then continued.

"I had a family once too." Now more guardedly, her voice lowered. "Well, at least a husband…" She looked at me for what appeared some form of confirmation. I nodded my head to certify that I was onboard for the story which by then I realized must be either very painful, or some form of military secret.

"We lived here, ran the place for years and were happy; oh, I guess in love too." She almost squirmed like a school girl. "He was such a hard worker, seems we seldom had time together except…to sleep."

Now she blushed, but continued. "It was winter, an icy-cold winter of deep snow and harsh winds, and he was helping uncouple a freight car on the rails, just out back of here."

Her head nodded toward the back of the lodge, where the rails still stood in rusty silence. "The engineer misread the brakeman's directions, the cars rolled back, Oscar was killed instantly."

Tears flowed unashamedly now and I was stuck for anything to say, to even attempt to assuage what must have been a most terrible moment in the life of this lovely, mature lady.

"I'm so sorry. I wish I hadn't made you feel like telling me this part. I hope you forgive my intrusion." I glanced at her face for any form of understanding.

"It was long ago." She gave me a slight nod. "Tell me about your weekend in the mountains."

With less than my original enthusiasm, I told her a brief replay of my two-day adventure and of plans to return soon for further treks into snow and rock. "I will return soon having enjoyed your comfortable hostel, warm fire, hot food and enthralling conversation."

I hoped my compliments would be received with a positive energy, but it was quite the opposite. In a most unexpected reaction, Edith very suddenly seemed remote, and quickly finishing her wine, excused herself and hastily left the room. I was left to puzzle over events which often befall us in life and how quickly fires can grow cold for no apparent reason.

I glanced about for further guests who might have been able to explain the sudden disappearance of our hostess, but aside from the elderly gentlemen apparently sleeping opposite the fireside from me, the place was deserted.

Embarrassed, and slightly troubled with the turn of events, I left what seemed to be the correct amount of money on the table plus a generous gratuity, and quietly grabbed my small pack and parka and reluctantly departed the abrupt chill of the Ruheplatz.

The snow was again falling outside but it seemed warmer after the unexpected cool within. I climbed into my rig, engaged gears and finished the uneventful downhill journey home. All too soon there would began yet another week of dispatching military aircraft ten hours a day.

As quite often happens, the following Saturday and Sunday found me dealing with chores, paperwork and the endless mending of climbing and camping gear; although not exactly a chore, as it typically preceded another trek into snow, rocks, mountains and trails.

At last, the following Friday, I was off work by two in the afternoon and well up the road to Berkhalden and Ausladen Peak. I had all intentions of stopping for warmth and refreshment at Ruheplatz, but in my frenzy to accomplish the trailhead, the hostel at Mitthausen passed by amidst a flurry of fresh snow and icy roads crunching rowdily beneath my impatient tires. Rather than turn back, I gave it a miss while planning to stop on my return downhill; by that time certain to crave warmth, food and attempt to salvage some communication with Edith.

Rather than the minimalist bivouac sack I frequently carried, I had elected to bring a small, one-man, all-season tent. Slightly larger and with the additional luxury of a small entry area, or vestibule, my nights would be vastly more comfortable.

The weather let go a slightly fiendish storm, including a snowfall measuring up to nine inches at the summit, and winds to pull one off the wall. As a result, mid-way through the following day's climbing agenda, I reluctantly returned to the vastly less exciting, albeit safer, confines of the tent and a peaceful, evening with a book, a hot meal and a small lantern.

My dinner consisted of reconstituted veggie soup, some hard cheese and crackers, a hardboiled egg, laced hot chocolate and resin and oatmeal cookies from a favorite bakery near the base. Properly filled, I found the peace of snow falling on nylon and winds shouting cautioning voices among nearby trees, a temperate balm to pull my mind away from the harsh, failed rope attempts of the afternoon. Presently my environment and I lapsed into a peaceful nocturnal slumber.

Morning arrived with a passion; the snowfall had intensified and the wind was well into double digits.

There would be no climbing today. In fact, I made the decision to take the hike out to the car early lest I become snowbound.

With guarded reluctance but few regrets, my return hike left me enjoying what scenery I could locate, often hidden by the driven snow which offered a frenzied attempt at disguising the ice-cold trail.

Arriving back at the trailhead, and clambering, gear and all, back inside my slightly-warmer machine, I attempted to crank it up. It sensed my reluctance to go back downhill to civilization, and at first refused to go into gear.

"Blast, now what?" I was cold, disappointed at the diminished opportunity for climbing activities over the weekend and somewhat worried too. *What if's* popped up like spring crocus, teaching me patience. However, after about a dozen attempts, things went right and machinery, gears, rubber, and snowbound highways found me caught up in the downhill crusade toward civilization, home and work. With a sudden glad heart and a well-placed grin, I realized there was something to look forward to; my second visit to Ruheplatz and a much-anticipated effort to correct whatever had gone wrong in my interchange with Edith.

There are times in life – we each have a shorter or longer list of them – when nothing can explain away the absolutely unreasoned events and their circumstances in the entire balance of things. What follows is topmost of my list of those illogical happenings.

Upon arrival at Ruheplatz, I was again escorted to a small table fireside and again was astonished at how few customers were in attendance. But then, it was a Saturday eve and perhaps that was never a busy time for this hostel. As before, there existed an elderly man, dressed for the cold and slouched, possibly asleep, in an overstuffed chair fireside. I was anxious to get warm, to enjoy another bowl of a wonderful home-cooked vegetable soup, and to visit with Edith.

As I attempt to narrate this portion of the story, I will endeavor to present it in a way which you can believe. I must inwardly struggle not to break down or become slightly irrational in the process.

I greeted the server, tall and rugged with a weathered face, almost too much hair for "food service" help and a stammer. I spoke calmly as I ordered soup, bread, coffee and apple pie for a dessert. Then, when finished ordering I very calmly asked, "Is Edith working tonight?" and things seemed to just go to pieces.

"What did you say? Edith? Did you ask if Edith is working?" He looked slightly, well, horrified. "How do you know Edith? Why do you ask for her?"

I was dumbfounded. What on earth had I done? I walked into a slightly familiar bistro, ordered some food and asked if the lady who had served me two weeks prior was working that night.

"I, that is, well…two weeks ago when she served me here…"

"What the hell are you talking about, two weeks?" He became almost hysterical, waved his arms and yelled, "Edith, Edith, what the…" He was a wild man.

From the back room a lady, more my own age, appeared and talked calmly to the server who took the menu card, the order sheet while he, still distraught and waving agitatedly, left the room. She was very much the dusty-blond and freckles and long stockings type, She gestured to the only other chair at my table and asked if she could join me.

"Of course, and I'm sorry. What did I say to set him off so?"

She introduced herself as Lynda, looked at my face steadily, and with a slightly inquisitive tension forced me to glance away.

"You asked about Edith, and you say you met her here as your server a week or so past?" She was slightly nervous and spoke each word with a slow not quite right pause, such as a child learning to speak a language or a musician tackling a new piece of music.

"That's all I did. I enjoyed conversation with her two weeks ago as she waited on my table." I took a breath and felt like I must hurry lest she lash out in anger, or jump up and run.

"She talked about her work with the railroad, about her deceased husband who was also a railroad worker. Brakeman, I believe. She sat right there," I indicated the very chair in which Lynda now sat.

I continued, slowly as if coaching a small child. "She sat there and enjoyed a glass of wine. I remembered her, enjoyed our time together and decided to come back, to eat and delight in more conversation with her. Why is that apparently so uncanny, such a problem either for you or the other waiter to understand, to accept?"

I felt the fires of inquisition crawling up my body, consuming me in what at first was just a slight worry and then, well then, in hot tongues of flame setting my entire self on fire with terror, almost fear for my life. What on earth was happening here?

"Sir, did you say your name was Eric? Well Eric, you see, that could not have happened. You could not have had any such discussion with Edith, at least not two weeks ago."

"Well, I am sure it was not three weeks ago, although I guess it may have been. Time moves so fast it seems." I was attempting to get things to work out, and they just refused to behave in such a manner.

"Eric, you could not have had that conversation with Edith two, three weeks even two or three years ago. Edith Hatcher, the lady married to that man sitting over there fireside, well, she died in a railroad accident 25 years ago this very night!"

One would think that she would have become calmer after getting all of that drama off of her mind and into mine. It had just the opposite effect, she seemed to come completely separated from her senses.

"Did I say died?" Shouting now with hands gesturing wildly, words flying like sticky sputum from her curled lips. "She vanished in a railroad accident, caught in a coupling catastrophe as the train pulled forward. She was apparently wedged between two freight cars. It was during a heavy snowfall and in the calamity she was not missed for some time, hours I would guess."

She checked to see if I was paying attention, maybe to see how the story was touching me. I was very linked, like the railroad cars.

She continued. "Eventually the cry went up, "Where is Edith?" Then the search began, but by then her body had been dragged for, well probably for miles. It must have come apart over the 200 Meter tall Hinderloc Bridge and was shoved, in pieces, down between the crossties, to land over 600 feet below. What did survive would have been eaten by wolves or bears!"

Now she sat back and looked at me for any form of response, for some degree of understanding, for whatever closure a stranger might offer as to such events taking place those many years past. I had nothing, nothing at all to offer. I was exhausted, as if from a hard climb, a long run, a beating even. I was drained and slumped back in my chair, not unlike the old man who still quietly snoozed in his fireside chair.

She continued in a frantically hoarse whisper. "That man, whom you see slumped in the chair warming himself by the fireside, that's Oscar, and he was her husband. After her death, he went totally insane, ran about raving, and eventually grabbed the station gun, kept for use against bears, wolves, possible railroad bandits. But anyway, he grabbed it and in a fit of madness, he shot the agent, the engineer, the conductor, turned the gun on himself and he died also."

She sat slumped down in the chair, but obviously was not finished, and a good thing too…I was nothing if very uncomfortable realizing that I was sitting in a room with a man who supposedly died 25 years earlier!

"Oscar had a huge financial interest in the whole berg of Mitthausen, nest -egged over many years and as such he had a codicil in his will which held sway over much of what happened the days following that terrible event."

This time when she paused it was to gain my full attention as she leaned across the table, grabbed one of my shaking hands in a firm grasp, and looked me full in the face with something of a mixture of horror and anger.

"In his will he left his worldly belongings, including a large fortune in funds stashed away, to the city of Mitthausen and to this hostel in particular."

I stabilized my emotions, focused on her gaunt stare and attempted to establish some form of realistic communication.

"Yes, I get it. And is that such a harsh demand?"

It appeared that his final request was as simple as, *Keep the place going and I'll fund it in my last will.*

I don't get it at all. Or at least not quite yet, I didn't.

"You don't understand, do you? You just don't get the picture."

She got up close to my face then and fairly cried, "Here, look carefully at that man, there, the one sitting slightly sprawled in the chair by the fire; same place you saw him two weeks ago, where he sits tonight, where he will be in a week, three weeks, three years. Look at him all you wish…he's dead! That's a stuffed corpse and his final will was that he sit there in solemn respect for his lost wife; for Edith, forever waiting for Edith!"

Upon arrival home that night, I was aghast to realize upon looking in my bathroom mirror, that my hair had turned completely white!

THE THIRD HOLE

Morning

"There, finished, and good riddance I say. That's the last of them finished and the last we've got to see of them too, I hope."

The sweltering mountain-top sun selected the perspiring armor-clad soldier in its' direct ray, displayed him in sloppy exhibition and caught him resting on his shovel. His face exposed how out of shape he was for digging holes and moving dirt about. He was red, sweating and not nearly as puffed up as he typically was when surrounded by cool breezes, lovely ladies in veils and tall glasses of wine.

"Gather those tools you men. Don't leave a lot of junk scattered about. This is supposed to be a royal event. A king will be here today they say, and to that I say 'Ha'."

The centurion smirked, and wiped sweat from a still-reddened face. "King, my word. No king will be atop this hill today, much less adorning that cross."

This man was used to having those under him respond without a second thought. "Get a move on and finish up here; I'll be downhill for a drink."

He strode off and left the two men alone to finish the task. They were workers, had no imagination, and felt vastly less than a small pinch of concern for the goings on up that hill, save perhaps their own interests of getting back to a cooler spot in the village below.

Midday

At last, they gave me something to drink. Well, it was liquid and within reach of my agape and burning mouth; a drink though? It tasted of gall, bitter. A punishment it was, rather than a quench; a punishment rather than a reward for my pleas, I suspect.

Not an hour earlier I had listened to the judgment, the final decree, and the barometer of my destiny.

"Guilty, guilty, guilty," *And directly after, they had decided on the penalty for my deeds, for my guilt. Again the voices rose in merged agreement; not imprisonment, no penal servitude, not even cast out into exile; the aggregate voice pronounced my punishment..." Death!*

"Kill him, kill him!" Once would have worked, repetition only spelled out the lust of the crowd and, united in their voices, they were prolific.

My crime? Well, I was overzealous, claimed to be a peacemaker, healed the flesh as well as the spirit, and did not hold with the habits of the wealthy, and powerful. I was a misfit.

The accusers were the proletariat, those whom I had sought to serve, as well as the worshipers of the idols, criminals and such. Mindful of their mission, they were united in finding a scapegoat and opted for a little known local medicine man dealing more with the maladies of spirit than the ailments of the flesh. My practice ultimately would advance beyond 2000 years and be known worldwide; although at that time it was brief by chronology and extended possibly 200 miles.

Would my associates be gathered up from the darkened corners of our village and sentenced also? I doubted that and hoped with all my heart for their safety. While they were few in number their loyalty sparkled in the sunlight, but perish the thought if nighttime fell hard on them. Most, under the strain of a harassed friend would falter and fail in their devotion. One failed over the lust for thirty pieces of silver and in the end sold me for a few pieces of the soft metal.

"Please, get me something to drink; my mouth is so dry." Fallen on deaf ears; worse, disinterest and a warped mentality marked them as adversaries.

The punishment was going to be slow. It was designed that way. We, three of us now, were to be examples to the crowd. Punishment is meant to both reward the justly deserving and dissuade those with a thirst for crime. Gathered together to observe, the shock might staunch the flow of crime in the novice; little chance existed to trample haughty hopes of lifetime perpetrators.

No one received a more unjust punishment than the innocent gathered by a chance encounter and forced to observe the ritual. But the streets that day were lined mostly with those who knew this was right for my punishment. They strutted about free from sin and corruption. These were the blameless; after all they had been inside the temple, paid their fee, and sallied forth unblemished.

The night before had been a trial in itself. Although my body remained free my spirit became shackled as darkness overtook the hot desert countryside. Black of night matched my darker spirits and while my Father had stood guard over my emotional cadence, I was aware of a creeping growth of accusers approaching as I kept midnight vigil in that gloomy and solitary garden.

I had tried to fit in. My functions had been to direct, to correct, to counsel and to repair. Healing of the flesh took vast sums of faith. I said, "Get up and walk" to the cripple; does he? Dare he? But he can. Repairs to the mind required faith beyond that of touch. Inside the mind dwells weakness more bountiful than a withered hand, or a body wracked with leprosy.

"Can you make me whole again?" That question challenged higher-level problem solving; whole from within, a tongue free from lying, or just a new leg or eyes that could see? I had addressed them all. Most were idle hopes instilled with temporary faith. I sympathized with them, made bodily changes and helped spirits heal and become whole again.

Climbing this mountain before me would grant none of the usual benefits of such a stone-strewn ascent to the altitudes. On any day one may attack that same hill and approach the warm sky, free oneself from the noise of the city below, breathe fresher air, and come closer to God's tranquility. Not so with my trudge that day. All I had to look forward to at the zenith of my efforts was...death! I was going to die and had to climb a steep mountain in order to accomplish that abhorrent end. The effort alone, along with the lumber I had to tolerate, would revenge a weaker man. But I was a teacher, leader, messiah and savior; albeit a 'criminal,' hence surely above pain and suffering. But my flesh, couldn't it feel the rifting and rending of bone and sinew too? My spirit unenthusiastically abides the pain of contempt and the anticipation of separation from my students, my friends and, perhaps even my Father.

The roadside was crowded, and not with old friends and acquaintances either. This rebel band was as anxious for a crucifixion as were my judges. Three of us hiked up that blemish in history called Mt. Golgotha, place of skulls, mount of our death. Three men with just one thing in common, all condemned: by a judge, by a society, by the law of the land; condemned to death in the most demeaning manner – crucifixion!

We bore up under the heat of a hostile midday sun, sweltering beneath massive beamed hangers, curses and jeers of the crowd. We bore up, stumbled, crawled onward, and fell only to be forced up again.

I could climb no longer and fell heavily to the ground, my back crushed beneath the weight of the cross which I had to bear to the hilltop, site of my transition, that cross of my own death.

"Here, you. take this cross," the voice scratched across the rumble of the crowd and the scrape of the timber along the road. Grunts and more shouting, "You, carry it now, get hold of it man Move, Move!"

Simon, a believer, a random man from the crowd, was selected by an armored Roman soldier to bear my burden as I had chosen to bear the entire burden of all of mankind. He hardly flinched at the taste of that whip, and, bending down 'neath the weight, he began moving onward, upward. The look on his face was not terror, fear or hate. He was not, I realized, experiencing his first ever walk with the Christ, while I, released from that portion, lurched ahead with the other two prisoners.

Approaching the summit it grew windy as a deep tone of purple and gray filled the heavens, as though someone had tossed a royal cape over the scenario. The hill top gave way to a cropped and rocky crest, liken to a rough sea during a heavy storm, and not so very contrasting came the certain pinnacle of my life upon this earthly place.

I attacked the remainder of that hill one step at a time, reluctant to be dead, never more uncertain of the plan for which I came to earth a few years ago, but destined to leave in just such a manner. I edged up those stone and soil palisades headed for pain, horror and the end of life; life as I knew it.

There, up ahead I could make it out, the site they had selected... over there. Three holes bored into the earth's face; one hole set apart and prepared to place on high, yet cast down into death...me, the son of God, who created that very earth. There, can you see, that spot, right there? It will have no fame, will not have an enduring effect on the course of the surroundings: hillside, hole drilled down into the earth's face, thrust up timbers, all shall pass away. The lasting thing, that which will preserve against time eternal, that for which mankind will cry out, reach up toward, dip low to worship and revere, that one, suffering and dying, yet returning too, that Son of God most high who must die now, will last. He will last forever.

Afternoon

The crowd had grown by that time, saturating the hillside with the idle curious, some doubtful, a few new followers of the King; and what a king by that time.

The "crown" made of torturous thorns, was embedded into my bleeding skull, pushed firmly down into hair and skin and seated into soft areas about the temples. Whip marks striped my back, my garment had become simply a rag soaked with the bloody sweat-crusted splinters from the timbers.

What of those timbers, laid down now by the innocent surrogate: massive beams, lashed and nailed. They slumped silently on the trodden soil awaiting my enduring frame, their innocent posture formatted to rid me of any remaining dignity, waiting for the short conclusive drop into that third hole bored into the earth.

Daylight was growing dimmer, darkness at midday; odd how artistically chiaroscuro the day had become. Odd and yet foretold, anticipated yet dreaded.

I was hauled to those timbers, dragged and wedged down and then…then the horrid iron spikes! Almost as though admiring a newborn baby, they were individually held aloft for approval by the gathered multitudes.

And approval they received too.

"Crucify them! Kill them! Do it now!" No amount of love wasted here, save my lofty parents' passion for the completion of what is planned, ordained, and to come.

The prophecy fulfilled and as such I must…but not that, surely not…death! "My Father I plead with you, but not my will, rather, thine own be done."

The others first, and oh the screams, curses, and pleas they offered up to mute and uncaring afternoon air; not uttered to the Lord God. No, rather just entreaties for help, release, even to be killed quickly. This death was not to be quick, the very nature of a death titled *crucifixion* was slow torture; it was saved for hardened criminals and would-be kings, I guess.

"Now for this one," arrogantly blasted words from the guard, "King of the Jews. I'm certain if he were any form of king someone would have released him by now."

The sanctimonious guard smirked and continued with words more spit than speech.

"King Jesus, where is your hope now? Most certainly your cries will vanish as the pleas of the other two, taken up into the air above and forgotten."

He and the others grabbed my arms and stretched them wide. Wider still.

Then, as knotted tendons snapped, they attached the agonizing nails to reluctantly outstretched palms.

As with rejoicing, once those lush green palms had been laid down on cold earth to welcome this King of Kings. Now this same King faced a detested torture as his own fleshly palms reluctantly accepted a unity with heartless beams, fixed by the agonizing chiseling into feeling skin of cold and uncaring spikes driven to bleed the King of all mankind for the salvation of all mankind.

Slam!

"Oh my father, oh please."

Slam!

"Oh no, no, please!"

Slam!

"There, one side done, quickly, the other side. I need to leave. This day has turned cold and dark, frightfully so." The Roman guard did not like the outlook, speaking metaphorically most certainly

Slam!

"Father, where are you now?"

"Don't cry out to someone who will not listen, who doesn't exist.

Your father is not here. What do you think, that he would walk up the hill for a look?"

The soldiers lifted the cross up and the pain in my spiked wrists was excruciating. I suspect I passed out. When next I was aware they were driving a single spike into my crossed ankles.

Slam, slam, slam!

"Oh no, no, my Father, why have you forgotten your son?"

"Here, get this one up into the air and dropped into that empty third hole. Drop it hard. I don't want to pick this rack up again; way too heavy." His voice, almost arrogant, yet lazy - disinterest revealed his attitude – be done with it and be gone from that place.

Thud!

The third hole was no longer empty and useless. The mission for which it was commissioned, designed and bored into indifferent earth was at last realized. The third cross, central of the three and slightly raised above the rest, fell into that awful gash in the face of mother earth with all the ceremony of a dirt clod. But, eventually the world-wide impact would outshine all the stars and the suns in all the universes in existence. That hole held the cross of the Lord Jesus Christ, the cross that took from mankind for all time the face and figure of the one who took forgiveness and hope among sinners, healed the sick, changed and forgave thieves and set prisoners free. The cross which reduced every hope of mankind to a single dead body and removed that Christ from the earthly throne. But – gone forever?

It had grown darker, colder and now had begun to rain. My pain was unbearable and I continued to cry out to my heavenly father. My voice was echoed by those of the two thieves beside me. They screamed and shouted to the crowd, yelled curses to all around them. One turned to me and begged in an astonishingly calm voice,

"Help me..." In faltering words both pleading and questioning he implored, "Will you not save yourself if you are the Christ? Then please, save me!"

His voice calmed my pain, changed my cries to reassuring words; words to answer his pleas, to assuage him in his final hours.

"Truly, I tell you that today you will be with me in paradise."

As darkness and violence in the heavens resumed with the return of my agony, I realized death's closeness and certainty. It was then that the guards announced their plans to hasten our end.

"Here, you two, take these stakes and shatter their legs." He gave the vile job to others, not wanting to soil his own hands and character with the assured death knell of the three. "The weight on their arms and wrists will increase their pain, reduce their breathing, and death will rush to take them."

He was a monster; dressed like a Roman soldier but a monster just the same; and yet, as with all of mankind, worthy of forgiveness. He went about fulfilling orders given him, as I received my orders from a loving heavenly father and forgave even the soldiers of their sins.

The soldiers watched in amusement. "Those two are clinging to life while the 'King' is dying, even now. I suspect death has found in him little resistance; he is going limp, and look how he flops about. No need waste efforts cracking his legs. He won't be around much longer."

The chilled soldiers were huddled beneath a piece of clothing cast off from one of the three. As individuals they lacked the confidence and strength they garnered from their small group. The captain spoke slowly now, as the cold took his spirit, shook his courage.

"How I wish the other two would hurry up. I want to get away from this place, this cold, this rain."

Truth be known his courage failed with what his painful smites and insults failed to take from me.

I raised my sagging eyes to the sky, heaven, my Father and watched rain drops fill the darkened evening, saw them dance across the crust of the earth's face, filling gullies with heaven's tears in a futile attempt to remove from the site the full impact if such a deed, lashing both wind and rainfall against the moment in history most certainly responsible for the ending and beginning of belief, hope and faith in such as that day's death on the cross of scorn of one Jesus of Nazareth.

"My God, my Father, it is finished. I come to you."

"Look, he's still talking to his father." Not too cold to continue his mocking tone, the guard watched Christ in his final moments, watched as His face shone with love and forgiveness, not hatred; with pity, not anger; with anguish but never retaliation.

In a startled voice the guard asked the darkened day, "I wonder, could he actually be some form of a king? Could all this be true, what they say about him. Have we just killed the true son of God?"

They smashed the legs of the other two but Christ was already finished. Soon all three had left behind the vanishing crowd, soaking soldiers and the sad few who had gathered to mourn the loss of their friend, the leader, their Christ.

In his final orders, prior to a quick and subdued slog off down the hill the Roman ordered, "Give the body of this King to those women for burial. The other two, take them to a cave." All arrogance was vanished from his voice, his countenance held little of the haughtiness of earlier in the day. He shrugged off his feelings as a reaction to the cold and rain and retired to visit a local wine shop where even that did not remove his feeling of having perhaps been a part of a momentous error in judgement.

"But I was following orders…" he attempted to reassure himself. Later that night, alone in his chambers, he took his own life.

Eventually, the small band of followers removed Christ's body and carried it off for burial in a borrowed tomb. To those gathered, with waning faith it would appear he was simply a forgotten man, a man facing nothing; a dead man.

Evening

As depressing rain continued to fall from heaven, and tears dropped from sad-eyed mourners, the waters combined to fill the holes on Calvary. Nearby, the linen-wrapped body of Jesus was placed in the borrowed tomb and a stone closed the entry. Back atop the hill, rain finally filled the three holes to overflowing. Site of the final hours of the two thieves, the holes which had held their crosses soon vanished. Somber witness to suffering and death, the third hole, having housed the crucifix of Jesus quickly overflowed and disappeared. The timbers of his agony and earthly death were never again to be seen. All evidence of the agonizing event was swept cleanly from the mountaintop and soon enough from the eyes, minds, and hearts of the receding crowd of mourners; some believers, most doubters.

What next?

My recent death was not to last. On the third day I rose, visited friends and ascended to the Father to finish the work I came to do.

There are bodies to heal, spirits and minds to cleanse, baptisms, births, deaths and Bible teachings to carry out worldwide.

And you, do you doubt I am here?

Look at a sunset, a sunrise, watch the ebb and flow of the tides, the shifting of heavenly bodies. Watch a child grow and develop into a fine young person. Be there for a birth, and a death as well.

Are you part of God's great plan?

"You are."

The last teaching I gave, the Great Commission, "Go and preach my word to all the earth as it must be done; for only then shall I come again."

NAPA DUMPSTER KING

A steaming, vanilla-infused dark roast restored my core temperature following a cold night's security patrol and only slightly warmer morning swim.

Comfortable, warm, and tree-side in a scented, Christmas-decorated Starbucks, I sank deep into a soft, well-worn leather chair, hot drink and book in hand, allowing last night's patrol in and out of Napa's Laurel Street area to vanish with night's fading gloom and winking streetlights.

Now, if my favorite morning digs would remain quiet for a few revered minutes, I could relish how a hot drink can work a mind adjustment on valued reading time.

My mug steamed, my vision dropped to half-mast, I indulged in a wintertime novel from the pen of my favorite author, while the lights on the tree murmured of *Good Will to Mankind*. Time dawdled by, the level of my mug sank and the words obediently meandered across the pages.

Rudely, the trance-like atmosphere surrendered to tinkling icicles as the door swept aside any semblance of calm, and ushered in a five a.m. cold-embracing rain and a bad extra for Father Christmas: enter the Napa Dumpster King.

"Rudy" was resplendent in old burlap, a pair of very mismatched work boots, different in color, one black the other brown, different in size as one flopped loosely with each step, and both wrapped in layers of river-bottom mud and slime. He had acquired a massive cape of some "Star Wars" form and it enveloped him from head to foot, but was missing a large portion of the back, which from the looks of it, had vanished in some campfire misadventure. If a barber had ever visited any part of his head it had been in years past and the job had been more in the manner of a punishment for the observer than grooming for the victim. To complete the ensemble, Rudy wore grease, mud, grime and … blood, on most exposed flesh, and carried more filth under his nails than many *John Deere* excavators encountered in a lifetime.

Bottom line: he was more "stuff" than person.

He stopped upon entry and belched with the force of an Aleutian Island gale, shook his head as acknowledgement of his achievement, and mooched across the floor stones to the nearest black and chrome trash receptacle.

"Alas, there you are!"

He had our gathered attention now.

He rummaged into the bowels of the trash can and proudly held aloft a still warm, disappointedly empty venti cup of some customer's recent delight. Rudy ripped off the lid and surveyed his treasure with all the finesse of a hobbled elephant in a three-legged race.

"Ahhh, my darling why did you hide?"

He shook the empty container as his eyes searched the interior for some form of…life?

"My love, my life. Why did you leave me? Why did you run away?"

Now he had the full, focused attention of each of the early morning crossword puzzle junkies, iPhone, iPad, and Wall Street Journal students. I joined in the show. I had no choice really, as Rudy was about three steps away and I writhed 'neath a full olfactory smorgasbord: sweat, cooking oils, urine, a rotting decay-tainted garb and hints of unnamed animal leavings. He continued the show.

"My darling, so much time has passed," his voice wavered only slightly then continued in full timber. "You lusted after others, after a better life, and yet here you are in nocturnal languish revisiting our old haunts, traveling where we traveled, hibernating amid crumpled napkins, sticky wrappers and cups sucked dry by the very proletariat we rated well below our own class. Housed, I discover you amidst trash and debris rejected by yourself as no longer good enough, hitherto home to us as we braved those endless seasons of steaming summers in desert golf clubs and frigid winters at ski resorts."

At this point he achieved full operatic tenor and fairly danced in circles of ever increasing panorama as he waved about his "lost love" spinning and tossing "her" in upward spirals. His "darling" spun higher and higher into the air above our upturned faces as we remained in full euphoria.

Rudy continued. "Here you are in life's rubbish, litter, refuse and trash!" He spit that last word out with nothing short of disdain and passion.

At this point, he erupted into a falsetto of such magnitude as to gather from the icy dripping patio, his fellows whose morning dip into soggy trash bins had gained them each their dawn's early lust of much-cherished items: cups yet harboring brownish sips of coffee and sour milk, crusty ends of rancid buns, nice bits of unbitten, overdone cookies and burnt butts of soggy cigarettes. Into the fray and melee doddered the elderly, the lame, the halt and blind, street bound or fresh from their 500SL Mercedes, they arrived, all attracted by a frantic fanatic in a frustrated freak show of mind and mania. Rudy gave them all his finest closing act and curtain call:

> "Babe, ah Babe how I yet lust for all the cherished moments we spent in alleyways of slush, filth, empty bottles and tossed-aside charred chicken bones over sticky noodles of some milky pasta dish. Such as we shared can't be replaced nor laid aside; ours was a unity of mind, character and spirit meant to last a lifetime, till death us do part."

> He was again tossing "Babe" into the air in higher and higher cascades of acrobatic contortions.

> "Now I pledge my troth yet again to you my love, my lust, my all; I give you back to me as partner forever and cast you upward into orbital heights of love and heaven's lasting care."

With this Rudy gave "Babe" the finishing fling upward in endless spirals, into dim recesses of slightly smoky attic spaces well above our heads, upward into…the spinning ceiling fans!

Whack, whack, chop and slash, sliver, and sliver, and sliver.

It was finished. Gravity took over and the shaved remains of Rudy's "Babe" rained down on us as the gentle snows of winter's first breath plants lightly those drought quenching flakes of frozen beauty upon pines, thirsty mountain boulders and dried paths of fallen needles.

"The snow doesn't give a soft white dam upon whom it falls." (e.e. Cummings)
She baptized us in a white coat of tender flakes, and brought to the morning a somber peace, not beforehand, nor since vested upon that robustly scented collection of morning caffeine worshipers. Calm settled, newspapers rustled, electronics took back the distracted faces of those entombed by their 2x3-inch screens.

I dropped back into my chair with no shortage of hesitation. There was something holding us each hostage, as the unsettled atmosphere hovered over the oblivious multitudes, each huddled in their own shells and each accepting in greater or lesser degrees the implication of the recent emotional outburst and resulting snowfall.

I braved a sip of my cooling latte and glanced about.

He was still there, big as life and in no shortage of social impact, hunched in an emotional hover over the crumbs brave enough to remain, in a gentle flutter about the paving stones of the coffee house. He spoke words in a voice now impacted by all that had occurred, by his loss and gain, and by what might just have been a social statement contained within the disguise of a social-outcast hulk.

"As I came into your comfy domain this morning, I noticed you blanch and drop deeper into your snug safe sofas and leather chairs. I sensed your disgust and disdain for my lavish gown and odor of another life style."

Rudy glanced about to ascertain whether or not he had an audience, and recognizing a full house he continued.

"Living next to me won't diminish your social status any. Neither need you fear, if you chance to stand beside me; my poorness will not rub off on you."

He seemed to stand a bit taller at that plug.

"I may as well have arrived into your private midst behind the wheel of an Aston Martin, bedizened with Tiffany trinkets while garbed in an Ermenegildo Zegna suit and flashing a Mercier watch. It's your ensemble of closely-guarded society you seek to protect from the outsiders in your very midst. Well, I am here to tell you that, today I stand in your midst, an ordinary citizen, slightly covered in the muck and slime cast off by the very society you live among. Today I am an ordinary citizen. Nothing more, nothing less. However, as of 12 noon on Friday, January 20th," he paused to rip off the horrid mask disguising his mass-media familiar face. "As of that date, I am your next president of the United States. I am Donald Trump!"

He walked out of the room and into our lives, and we, the voters, were we so inclined, were about to place our single check mark for or against it.

Now, had this been the actual, soon-to-be President Donald Trump, or was it some dumpster king with a disguise beneath his disguise?

Next time you see him, go ahead and ask.